MURDER IN THE GARDENS

PENELOPE BANKS MURDER MYSTERIES

COLETTE CLARK

DESCRIPTION

You are cordially invited to the grand opening of the Japanese Tea Gardens on the rooftop of the Grand Opal Hotel...

New York 1925
To celebrate its official opening, the Grand Opal Hotel is hosting an exclusive party for the *crème de la crème* of New York society, to be held in its newly completed rooftop Japanese Tea Gardens.

Jiro Ishida, the gardens' designer is *l'homme du moment*. Everyone is clamoring for his services to recreate the latest trend in garden aesthetic.

Which is why it's a surprise when he turns up dead in the koi pond.

Once again, Penelope "Pen" Banks is on the case, if only to solve a murder the owner of the hotel and several of its wealthy guests would rather see buried beneath the bonsai trees.

Murder in the Gardens **is the fourth book in the Penelope Banks Mystery series set in 1920s New York. The enjoyment of a historical mystery combined with the excitement and daring of New York during Prohibition and the Jazz Age.**

ROOFTOP GARDEN MAP

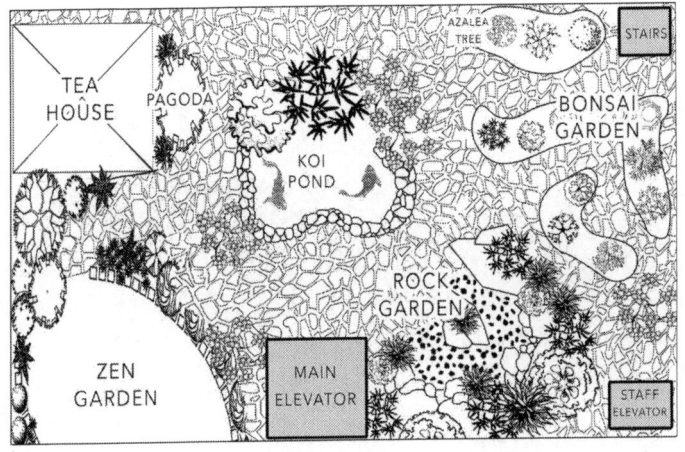

CHAPTER ONE

"You wouldn't happen to have anything to make this a little more...*criminal*, would you?" Penelope "Pen" Banks asked.

The young waiter was handsome enough, tall and well-built. However, it was the devilish grin that appeared on his face that ignited a flame of interest in her.

"I think I can help you out," he said, eyeing the glass she had lifted toward him. "Meet me inside the pagoda in about ten minutes."

"We *are* talking giggle juice, no?" Pen confirmed, a smirk appearing on her lips. She had mostly been teasing with her original suggestion, but now it seemed like this young fellow might be able to satisfy her wanton desires after all.

"I'm willing to accommodate any of your needs, ma'am." He arched an eyebrow that left that statement open to interpretation, which she thought was rather forward of him. Then again, she had opened the door to something wicked in the first place.

"I think I'll settle for sins of the liquid variety, thank

you." Penelope's smile turned slightly sardonic, causing him to chuckle.

Pen watched him continue to serve the last of the drinks on his tray—sadly limited to ginger ale and punch. Prohibition had cast such a dull net over society. That was probably why the crowd around her was the bluenosed sort, despite the public's curiosity about the new gardens around her.

On a Saturday night, most people Penelope's age or younger would more likely be at a party or speakeasy where the cocktails were free-flowing. At twenty-four, Pen was among the youngest attendees. She had allowed her fascination to trump her need for an exciting night or a stiff drink.

It was the official opening of the Grand Opal Hotel, specifically the rooftop gardens. Located on 5th Avenue near the southeast corner of Central Park, it was heralded to be one of the finest modern luxury hotels New York City had to offer. The event was being held in the newly completed gardens on the roof. After tonight, when the Opal Tea Room opened, there would be small tables set up along the pathways and inside the tea house. Anyone who was anyone had come out to view the unveiling of the masterpiece before then. It was a work of art that would have made Michelangelo himself weep.

The entire theme was Japanese, which had suddenly blossomed into vogue over the past few years. The designer, Jiro Ishida, had completed a design for the Brooklyn Botanical Gardens, which Penelope had admired last year.

Having seen the magic Mr. Ishida had worked in Brooklyn, she had been curious about what he could do with the much smaller square footage of this hotel.

She had not been disappointed.

"I don't get it," a woman whined nearby. "It's just…

white sand with a big rock in the middle. In my opinion, a garden needs flowers, or at least *something* green."

"I think that's the point, dear," the man with her said. "It's supposed to make you think, or calm down, or something like that. The designs in the sand represent this Zen business I think. Has to do with the Far East mentality. They have a different way of looking at the world, you know —sitting around thinking instead of doing. I tell ya, the Japanese will never be a serious contender on the world stage if they keep spending their time on hogwash like this, as interesting as it is to look at. We were right to limit how many of them come here. We need people who have a bit more mettle in them."

Whether any of that was true, Penelope had her doubts. Still, whatever calmness she'd felt just now, staring at the Zen garden, was decidedly ruined by their blathering.

She moved further along, around past the tea house working toward the furthest point of the roof. It was away from the most of the crowd and was called the Bonsai Garden. It was a lovely display with miniature trees set in large containers atop moss-covered stands. They were strategically situated among several plots of greenery and gray stones.

Penelope took a moment to peacefully breathe it all in. The mix of flora created an interesting scent in the air that wasn't exactly pleasant. Perhaps it was all the people about with their perfumes and cigarettes. It was still preferable to the usual smell of the city below them.

Here, the sound of chatter didn't ruin the mellow jazz music played by a small quartet situated in between the Tea House and the Zen garden. The night was clear and pleasant enough that the awnings that would eventually shield the mostly female clientele from the sun had been taken down.

"Oh, aren't they darling!" squealed a voice behind her.

It was grating enough to have Penelope wincing. She turned to find a young woman with a man twice her age. The woman was quite pretty with a brunette bob, heart-shaped face, and a *very* shapely figure that was nicely outlined by her black dress with tiny gold beads. It had a hemline that paid heed to the trend of inching higher and higher these days, though hers seemed to be well ahead of the pack, settling a good inch or so above her knees.

The man she was with was instantly recognizable to Penelope.

Bentley Green was currently one of the most famous architects in New York City. According to many sources, he was singlehandedly responsible for helping to modernize the aesthetic of the city from its glory days of the Gilded Age into something more fitting for the twentieth century.

He had been mentored by the infamous Stanford White whose architectural stamp was permanently etched onto this city from the Washington Square Park Arch to the second Madison Square Garden, which was sadly closing for renovation this year.

It seemed design wasn't all that Bentley had learned from his old mentor, a man who also had a taste for much younger women. It's what had eventually led to Stanford White's murder, a rather sordid and scandalous affair.

One would have thought Mr. Green would have taken that as a hint. Still, this young woman seemed to at least be of legal age. Still, old men like Bentley always seemed to have a side to them that was less than respectable.

"Look at this one, Benty, it's got pink flowers. Like a tree made just for a doll. I want one of my own!"

MURDER IN THE GARDENS

Bentley removed the small brown cigarette from his mouth to exhale and reply. "Not to worry, sweet pea, if things go according to plan, you'll soon have an entire garden of these magnificent little things at your disposal."

"Will they all be with pink flowers like this one? Oh! You should get a hundred of 'em for the show you said you were going to produce for me, Benty. Wouldn't that be the absolute bee's knees!" His date leaned in to study it more closely, then wrinkled her nose and pulled back. "Or at least ones that smell like roses or somethin'."

"And here I thought you didn't like flowers," he said with a teasing grin.

"On dresses silly-willy," she said in a baby voice, that had Pen rolling her eyes. "Besides that dress wasn't pink! So can you buy me one of these? Speaking of which, when is the show gonna—"

"Not now, Darlene, this is an important night for me. I can't get distracted."

"But—"

"Not now," he ordered.

"*Fine*," Darlene whined with an exaggerated pout.

Penelope was glad once Bentley led Darlene away so she could enjoy the space without that grating, high-pitched whine filling the air.

"Pathetic," muttered a man standing near the next plot of tiny trees. He noted Penelope turn to glance at him and met her with a dry look.

"Some people have no appreciation when it comes to the Far East. Trees for dolls? She should have her invitation revoked just for that. That one with *pink flowers* is an azalea species that is quite delicate, requiring constant care and attention. It's almost two hundred years old and worth hundreds, or at least *should* be. But what can you expect from the pedestrian classes? This is what comes from trying to bring culture to the masses. A precious, living artifact is reduced to a toy for children."

The man's demeanor was as snobbish as his words. He had a slight build that was clothed in a very well-tailored suit, with two gold cuff links. His dark hair was combed straight back which only highlighted his most striking feature, black eyebrows that formed two straight slashes above his blue eyes. They angled down toward his nose giving him a severe almost exotic look.

"Hiring Jiro was a stroke of genius, I'll grant you. He's become *l'homme du moment*, sadly. Yet another eastern aesthetic ruined by philistines. As you can see he's combined several different themes. A tea garden, *roji*, is quite different from the *karesansui*, near the entrance." Pen assumed he meant the Zen garden with beautifully raked white sand. "You might as well mix velvet with tweed, never mind the addition of this bonsai display, as impressive as most of the specimens are."

While it was interesting to put a proper Japanese name to things, Penelope thought he was wrong in how it worked together. She thought the result was beautiful, like entering a new and different world with each garden.

"Good for Mr. Ishida though. He won't want for work. Japanese gardens are—"

"No longer a fascination but a standard it would seem." His tone indicated that he was rather put out by this fact. As though it was a personal affront to him.

The last thing Penelope wanted was to get stuck in a conversation with someone so dour and pretentious, especially without the benefit of a sip of giggle juice. It reminded her that perhaps ten minutes had finally passed.

"I have to..." She gestured behind her and gave him a

tight smile before backing away. She walked further along into a picturesque scene filled with trees, shrubs, and rocks. It smelled of cloves, which was a nice touch, though she couldn't place the source. A bed of tiny pebbles ran through the center of this garden, mimicking a river that almost looked like the genuine thing.

She continued on, passing by the grating Darlene stomping her foot over something she was jealous about, which Bentley patently ignored. The pagoda was located back near the tea house. Despite the crowd of guests, Penelope took the long way around. It was a pleasant walk underneath Japanese maples, past bamboo trees, and most beautiful of all, the cherry blossom trees that were still in full bloom this time of year. If this was becoming standard as far as gardens went, she didn't see it as a problem.

Of course, the man of the hour himself, Jiro Ishida, wasn't too terrible to look at either. Penelope just now caught a glimpse of him as he stood talking to a pretty young woman near the furthest part of the Zen garden.

Jiro was quite a handsome man, well-built with pronounced cheekbones and sharp brows over intense eyes. His genius green thumb and eye for design made him all the more attractive. Tonight he was in a cream three-piece suit, looking quite debonaire.

The woman talking to him was close enough to make the two of them seem intimate. That's perhaps why the crowd—many here to meet him specifically, like Pen herself—kept their distance. The woman looked up at him with adoring eyes as she made some ardent plea. Jiro seemed torn as though he wanted to do what she was asking, but was hesitant. It was an intriguing enough picture that Penelope stopped out of curiosity, surprised she was the only one observing. A white woman and a Japanese man in a tableau that hinted they might be lovers should have certainly drawn eyes.

The more glaring distraction drawing everyone's eyes soon became apparent.

"Trees, bushes, sand, *and* water? That's the kind of thing that'd give a golfer like me nightmares! I might just have to drink something a bit stronger than this here ginger ale y'all are servin' to get some sleep tonight!"

A chorus of laughter came on the heels of that booming bit of jocularity. Penelope shifted her gaze away from Jiro and the woman to land on a man who seemed to have the kind of personality that created an orbit of its own. He was in front of the main attraction of the garden, a rocky waterfall spilling into a koi pond. It was set in the center of the gardens, visible as soon as guests stepped out of the elevator. Right now, a small crowd had gathered around the man, so she was only able to see a bit of him.

"It's a good thing I brought along some of my good ole Georgia homebrew, if you know what I mean." Pen wondered how much of this "home brew" he had imbibed before this event. Or perhaps this was just his personality, loud and obnoxious. "I think I'm definitely gonna need it. I see my Betty over there with Jiro, plottin' and plannin' a garden of her own for when we get back home. I don't know about all this bamboo and bonsai whatever. The only green I care about is the one I tee off on!"

At that statement, the woman with Jiro instantly stepped away from him and turned to face the man whose voice carried to every ear on the roof. Betty planted a smile on her face and walked over to join him, making her way through the crowd. She tucked into his right side readily enough, but even Penelope could see she was somewhat embarrassed by his bombastic nature. He seemed ready to wrap his arm around her delicate shoulder but got halfway and thought better of it, bringing it back down to his side. A smart man always knew when not to overstep his significant other's goodwill.

Well, that was all very interesting, Penelope thought as she continued on. She cast one last glance back at Jiro Ishida before he was swarmed by a crowd of admirers.

Penelope couldn't quite gauge what that expression on his face was, angry or frustrated, but she knew one thing for sure, he was upset about something.

CHAPTER TWO

Penelope continued toward the pagoda, squeezing through the crowd. Once there, she knocked on the only door.

The waiter opened it a peek, then gave her a grin. "Come on in."

"I certainly hope this wasn't some guise to get me alone inside. Those people out there can still hear me if I scream."

"Well, we can't have that," he said, again in such a way that made it seem like she was missing out on what else he had to offer.

Saucy boy.

She entered the small space, which turned out to be a cleverly disguised storage and gardening supply shed.

"How does a bit of Macallan whisky sound?"

"Impressive," Penelope responded, eyebrows raised in honest surprise. She had expected a bit of bathtub gin or some homemade hooch that would leave her gut rotting.

"Being that it meets with your approval...." He reached in between some boxes and underneath a canvas cloth.

"Ouch!" He hissed in pain as he pulled the bottle back

out. There were what looked like bloody claw marks showing through the ripped parts of his dress shirt. "I forgot about all the gardening tools back here."

"Well, they do say bootlegging is a dangerous business. I suppose I should give you extra for that," Penelope sympathized.

"Just one of the costs of doing business, ma'am. I can change into my backup shirt down in the basement later."

Pen dug into her small purse and pulled out a ten-dollar bill. "Is this enough to top me off? Just pour it into what's left of my punch."

He grinned back and plucked the money from her hand. It was an outrageous sum for what amounted to nothing more than a few fingers, as quality as the brand was. Still, she had to give it to him for knowing his clientele. No one in attendance on the roof was worth less than several hundred thousand dollars. The owners had priced the tickets to this event to weed out the "riff-raff" who probably wouldn't have been able to afford a room at this hotel anyway. Penelope herself was worth a few clams short of five million thanks to a generous gift left to her earlier that year by Agnes Sterling, a dearly departed friend of her deceased mother.

Pen took a sip of her impromptu cocktail and hummed in appreciation as the heat of it trickled down her throat.

"I could sell you the whole bottle for a few more of those tens."

"Smuggled under my dress, I presume?" she replied with a laugh.

"Come down to the staff rooms in the basement after this little shindig and I'll have it ready and waiting for you."

"We *are* talking about the Macallan, no?" she had to once again clarify.

He laughed. "Yes ma'am. Of course, there's also a nightly game of poker if you're interested."

Pen pulled the cup away from her lips and her eyes lit up. "You don't say!"

One side of his mouth hitched up with pleasant surprise. "You play?"

"I wouldn't call it playing so much as outright murder."

That earned her another laugh, much heartier this time. "Well then, I'll save you a seat."

"Do I at least get a name to write on your tombstone?"

"I'm Gary Garret."

She laughed. "Really?"

"Yes, I know, my parents were real comedians."

"Hello, Gary Garret, I'm Penelope Banks," she stuck out her hand.

"I should warn you, the group is a bit...colorful," he said in a considering manner as he shook her hand.

"Colorful? Is that a euphemism?"

"Euphemism?"

"Coded language."

"Ah, well what I mean is, as long as you ain't too picky about who you play cards with, you're in."

Penelope laughed. "You'd be surprised at who I've played cards with."

Once upon a time, illegally gambling on cards had been Pen's main source of income. She'd played with everyone, from notorious gangsters to upstanding businessmen to the kind of foul-mouthed barbarians that would have most ladies of decent society fainting. And they certainly weren't mutually exclusive.

Outside, Pen could hear the sound of the music stop, which meant that the presentation was set to begin. Since she had come specifically to hear Jiro Ishida speak about his design and process, she took that as her cue to leave.

"I suppose I'll see you later on tonight. I hope you have your last will and testament written, boy-o."

"Meet me by the staff elevator. And I wouldn't be too sure of myself if I was you. I'm pretty good at committing murder myself."

"We'll see about that," Pen said with a grin as she quietly opened the door and snuck back out into the crowd.

"Ladies and gentlemen, if I can please have your attention!" A man said into a microphone. At the eventual silence, he continued with his introduction.

"My name is Wendell Dickens, the hotel manager of the newly opened Grand Opal Hotel. Welcome!" There was a small round of applause before he continued. "A select few of you have already experienced the luxury and eye for detail our lovely little pearl in this city has to offer as the first official guests in the suites. I'm sure each of you will attest to the elegance future guests can expect now that the Grand Opal is officially open for business. This hotel is a unique..."

Penelope sighed, realizing that he intended to drone on in order to sell the hotel. After all, tonight was a grandiose advertisement for the hotel more than anything else. The gardens had been the perfect bait.

Only when a small round of applause sounded again, did she pay attention again. She sagged when she saw an older woman approach the small stage rather than Jiro Ishida, who remained standing to the side, still looking rather unhappy.

"I give you, Genevieve Walton, the owner of the Grand Opal Hotel!" Wendell announced with overt enthusiasm.

Jiro glowered, though he seemed to be more angry than

annoyed. His hard gaze fell on the woman as Wendell helped her up to the dais. Once there, she waved the manager off with irritation, the gold bells on the bracelets lining her arms tinkling.

Genevieve Walton seemed to be well into her fifties. She wore a white turban, and an unfortunate amount of white powder, rouge, and lipstick. Her white silk dress was more of an intricate robe, perhaps a nod to the Japanese theme of the hotel.

"Thank you, thank you," Genevieve said. She used a lot of hand gestures and impassioned facial expressions that caused Penelope to bite back a smile. It didn't take Pen long to realize that she wasn't the only one who had indulged in a tipple this evening. It was a wonder how the woman was able to stand on the small dais without toppling over.

"When I *first* conjured up the idea of a hotel that embraced the *ethos* and *aesthetics* of the Far East, specifically the Japanese, I was told it *simply* couldn't be done. No, no, Genevieve they said, you *must* be American! You *must* be British! You *must* be French! *No, no*, I responded! I had a vision, you see, one that..."

Penelope sighed, feeling her impatience set in. Not only was Genevieve's voice trilled and exaggerated, but she was also quite long-winded. It was obvious she intended to go on for a while and Penelope was glad she had decided to self-medicate beforehand. In retrospect, the whisky had been well worth the extravagant price.

Pen tuned out most of the speech and had sadly finished most of her drink by the time Genevieve came to a close and finally introduced the man of the hour. Penelope perked up at the sound of Jiro Ishida's name and focused her attention back toward the small stage.

There was a moment of panic as Genevieve tried stepping down from the dais and nearly succumbed to her intoxication. Wendell was quick to catch and help her down.

"Oh stop, you silly man! I'm perfectly capable," she protested, even though it was obvious she wasn't. Still, Wendell fussed and fawned over her.

Before Jiro took the stage, Genevieve quietly whispered something to him that had his jaw hardening. While the hotel's owner smiled in a tipsy sort of way Jiro was now seething.

Still, he managed a tight smile before stepping up onto the stage to the sound of applause, Penelope's included. As he looked out into the crowd, something like sadness came to his gaze. It steeled into a brief flash of resentment before he steadied it and began to speak.

Penelope had read that he had been born here in America thirty-five years ago before his parents returned to Japan while he was still a child. Hence his expertise in Japanese gardening. Still, he'd been back in America long enough to speak without too much of an accent.

It was obvious that Jiro was passionate about the subject, and was quite eloquent, mesmerizing even, in explaining things so that even a novice would understand it. Anyone who came away from this event without a deeper appreciation for Japanese Gardens either had no interest in the first place or simply wasn't paying attention.

When Jiro left the stage, he quickly hurried away before the crowd could pounce on him once again. He certainly wasn't doing a good job of ingratiating himself to potential clients tonight. But it seemed the poor man had something troubling his mind.

Penelope followed him with her eyes. They widened in curious surprise when he headed directly toward Gary, who had finally changed. Jiro appeared to be requesting something of him. Based on the way his eyes darted back and forth, it was something he didn't want anyone to know about.

Penelope wondered what illicit item Jiro was seeking out.

Gary seemed rather surprised by the request, but after a moment shrugged and nodded, then replied. Jiro seemed frustrated by the answer, though Pen couldn't say whether it was directed at Gary.

Jiro stormed off but was caught by Bentley Green who, rather rudely, grabbed his arm to pull him aside. He was rewarded with Jiro snapping at him, and gesturing out toward the gardens. He jerked his arm out of Bentley's grasp and stormed off. The architect's face went red with rage. He probably wasn't used to being so abruptly dismissed. He glared after Jiro, then directed that same wrath toward the garden, where the crowd still gathered, mostly around Genevieve Walton to congratulate her.

It seemed there was a lot of unspoken animosity floating in the air tonight despite the festivities. Animosity that seemed to be building toward something.

What that was, Penelope wasn't sure.

CHAPTER THREE

"I suppose my night is done," Penelope said to herself. She was just as disappointed by Jiro's departure as the rest of the crowd was. They also seemed to have the idea that they had no more reason to stay. Pen had been hoping to at least congratulate Mr. Ishida on his success.

Perhaps some other time.

All the better it wasn't tonight since Mr. Ishida certainly didn't seem to be in a celebratory mood. She wondered what it was he had asked of Gary but decided it wasn't any of her business.

She didn't want to leave with the rush of people who were now exiting. Besides, she wasn't going home, she had a poker game to attend. Instead, she lingered, enjoying the scenery until even the musicians were packing up their instruments for the night. Penelope had sensed a note of something eastern in the music they played. The proprietor of the Grand Opal Hotel certainly knew how to focus on the details.

Everything except making sure the main attraction, Jiro Ishida, was happy.

Penelope searched for Gary and couldn't find him. In fact, all of the waiters had disappeared along with the musicians. That was her cue to seek him out by the staff elevator located back near the garden with the pebbled stream.

Gary was already there, smoking a cigarette as he waited for her. He met her with a grin.

"So, you've chosen murder," he said, pushing the button to call the elevator.

"May the best *woman* win," she responded with an arched eyebrow.

After what seemed like forever, the doors opened and he gestured for her to enter first. It was large, big enough to accommodate a maid's cart or bellhop's trolley. However, the beautiful murals and gilded mirrors of the guest elevators were absent here.

"How did you get a job at this hotel?" she asked as the elevator slowly eked its way down.

"I knew a guy who knew a guy," he responded with an ambiguous smile. "I'm good at knowing people."

"So it would seem."

"I guess I have that kind of face," he said with an exaggerated smile. "There's a reason you asked me for your little dash of poison and not some other waiter, even if you were teasing at first. I know how to pick 'em. Something told me you might be someone I should know."

"Is that so?" Pen asked, slightly intrigued. She'd always been fascinated by people like this.

Her friend Lucille "Lulu" Simmons was like that. She sang jazz at the Peacock Club. She also helped procure the "medicinal" brandy for Penelope's older Cousin Cordelia. She was the reason for Penelope being in this elevator right now. Lulu had been the one to suggest Penelope start playing cards to make ends meet when she had been cut off by her wealthy father and forced to fend for herself. Lulu not only knew all the locations where a lucrative game could be played, but also which pockets were the deepest.

The peculiar way Penelope's mind worked—in which she could remember everything like a colorized film in her head—somehow helped her play cards and usually win. She hated the idea of taking advantage of a waiter, but something told her Gary had his own tricks up his sleeve when it came to winning at poker. She was too invested to turn back now.

"I could probably use a guy like you in my business."

"You? In business?"

"What? Did you think I was nothing more than a member of the idle rich?"

"Yeah," he retorted with a grin, making her laugh. "What is it you do?"

"Private investigation."

"You don't say?" He replied, impressed. "Hell, maybe I could use a dame like you instead. You any good?"

"I may have solved a few murders, and I don't just mean the poker-playing kind."

Now he was really impressed, whistling in approval.

"Speaking of murder, let me guess, you're the one who first suggested this game of cards after hours?"

He grinned. "I am the man who can make things happen. I always know a guy—or a gal."

Penelope laughed. "So, if I wanted to, say...sneak into the Emperor suite just to see what it looks like?"

"Please, at least give me something challenging. Even with *Madame* Walton residing there, I could make that happen easy. Everyone on staff has a copy of the master key."

Penelope teasingly slapped him on the arm. "Have you been inside?"

"I've been inside them all, and yeah, that one is grand. I don't know much about those Japanese but they sure know how to do things in style."

"Okay, then, something harder...." Penelope mused for a bit. "How about City Hall?"

"How about the White House?" He countered with one brow raised tauntingly.

"My, my, my, you really do know a guy—or a gal," Penelope said in wonder.

Now she was even more curious about what Jiro had been requesting of him.

They finally arrived at the basement level and Gary once again gestured for her to go first. This floor, dedicated to all things staff, was just as bare and utilitarian as the elevator was. The narrow hallways were a boring beige and lined with carts, open lockers revealing hotel uniforms, and shelves filled with hotel supplies. It was fairly bustling, seeing as the hotel was now somewhat open for business.

Gary led her all the way down, past the curious gazes of other staff until he reached a room labeled "entertainment." He knocked three times and it was opened by a man Penelope recognized from the band at the party. He nodded at Gary but came to a sudden pause when he got to Penelope behind him.

She could understand his hesitation. It was one thing to consort with a fellow staff member. It was another to do the same with a white woman of a certain class. All anyone had to do was look at Penelope in her pink, chiffon dress with floral embellishments and a feminine, gauzy cape attachment to know she was of that particular class.

"What's this? You bringing in top hats and tiaras down here? You trying to get us all in trouble?"

"Don't worry about her, Sam. She's copacetic."

"Oh, Gary says everything's *copacetic*," Sam retorted, his eyes sliding to Penelope with suspicion. "That don't necessarily make it so."

"Don't tell me you're worried about losing to a, how'd you put it, *tiara* such as myself?" Pen sassed with a sly look. "I guess I'll have to take my hundred clams to someone who can handle it."

"What's that about a hundred clams?" Someone behind him exclaimed. Another man she recognized from the band elbowed his way past Sam and met Penelope with a broad grin. Pen recognized him as the cello player. "Ignore my thoughtless associate here, he don't know the meaning of manners. Name's Thomas, and I am *very* pleased to meet your acquaintance, ma'am."

"Call me Penelope, and are we playing or not?"

"Music to my ears," he said with a grin. He nudged Sam further out of the way and opened the door wider for her. Sam still looked suspicious. Based on the way he eyed Pen and then Gary, she could see he'd make a formidable opponent.

"So, are we copacetic?" Gary whispered as he passed by Sam.

"We'll see," Sam said in a noncommittal voice.

Good, Pen hated when men treated her with kid gloves.

"Let the murder commence, boys," she said to the men already seated at the table in the middle of the room.

Two hours later, the room was filled with staff who had steadily trickled in over the course of the game. Maids, wait staff, bellhops, and more all craned their necks to see which of the remaining three players would collect the impressive pile of kale from the latest round.

It was down to Pen, Gary, and Sam, all of whom had already proven to be gifted players. Any hesitation Pen had about relieving them of their kale had diminished after a few rounds of her being taken, but good. Sam was a skilled, strategic player, smart but excitable; his tells were obvious. Gary, on the other hand, had perfected his reactions to both good and bad hands, such that she never knew what he held. Both of them made for an entertaining game.

"I raise you...twenty dollars," Gary said, eyeing both Pen and Sam. The sleeves of his shirt were rolled up exposing the cuts on his right arm.

Whistles and hums filled the air at the daring bid. Penelope had a pretty firm handle on both of her opponents by now and knew she couldn't win this round, even through bluffing.

"I fold," she said, tossing the pathetic hand she had down onto the table.

Sam and Gary eyed each other, subtle smiles coming to their lips. Pen wasn't sure why. She still had a few bits of kale left to play with for the next hand. On the other hand, Sam had won quite a bit earlier, but had gotten too bold for his cards and was now down to just twenty dollars, the same amount Gary had just raised.

He eyed Gary, studying him for clues to see what kind of hand he had. It was his flaw, which gave away too much. All it took was one subtle smirk from Gary to have him doubting himself. But there was a decent pile of money on the table that was too tempting for him to pass up.

"I see you."

"You sure? I'll give you a chance to pull out."

That ribbing was enough to embolden Sam. He threw his last bit of dough onto the pile then jerked his chin at Gary.

"Okay then," Gary said, laying his cards down to reveal a three-of-a-kind, queens. Quite impressive.

All one had to do was look at Sam to realize he had lost it all. He threw his cards down to reveal nothing more than two sevens.

"Damn it, Gary!" The hot-tempered saxophone player yelled. He shook a finger at his opponent. "You play too damn much!"

"That's the game, Sam. Stay outta the kitchen if you can't handle the heat," Gary said with a laugh as he scooped up his winnings.

Sam seemed ready to leap over the table but Thomas stopped him.

"He's right, man. You won last time, tonight you lost. Go walk it off."

Sam glowered, but shook off Thomas's restraining hand and stormed off, pushing through the staff that had been there to witness his defeat.

"Well, that's another murder out of the way, huh?" Gary said to Penelope with a grin.

"You're so good at this, Gary," one of the maids, Rosie, said with stars in her eyes. They flitted to the cuts on his arm, which gave him the look of a dangerous character, and Pen thought she might very well faint. "I had no idea what cards you had. You could be an actor like Rudolph Valentino."

"Gloria Swanson ain't got nothin' on you, doll," he said with a wink, making her giggle and blush.

He turned back to Penelope. "How's about we break with a little refreshment before the next round, that is, if you're still game to keep playing?"

"If you have that bottle of Macallan you promised, I'll pay for what's left and share it around."

"I saved it for you just in case."

That excited everyone and a happy chatter filled the room.

Penelope dug into her purse and pulled out fifty dollars and handed it to him. She was glad she'd come prepared tonight. It was no wonder gangsters and other bootleggers were becoming wealthy, the cost of illegal alcohol was…criminal.

Someone found a few of the glasses meant for hotel rooms, crystal tumblers with the Grand Opal Hotel logo etched into them. After pouring Pen a generous amount, Gary poured himself the same, then handed the bottle off to Thomas to divvy among everyone else as he saw fit.

It was a relaxed and vibrant atmosphere, the kind Penelope missed from her days hustling cards.

"So this owner, Genevieve Walton, she seems like a character."

Rosie, one of the maids giggled, which got her a knowing look from another maid, Leticia. Pen briefly wondered if they were sisters, both with dark hair and large brown eyes, and noticeably shapely figures, except Rosie was small compared to Leticia, at least in height.

"What's so funny about her?" Pen asked, eyeing them.

"Character ain't the half of it," Leticia said. "She's been living up in the Emperor Suite since before the hotel even opened. She's always wearin' that robe of hers, and watches us like a hawk whenever we're in there to clean. Like we're gonna steal something."

"When she ain't too ossified to stand, that is," Rosie added. "She's probably already out like a candle by now."

That got everyone laughing.

"She drinks something called sake, warm wine," Leticia said, wrinkling her nose.

Penelope bit back a smile, remembering the state of Miss Walton at the party. She felt a bit shameful indulging in gossip like this, but she knew that the staff always had their finger on the pulse of any establishment, and this hotel was fascinating, even though it had yet to officially open.

"What about Jiro Ishida? He didn't seem too happy tonight."

They all looked at each other, then shrugged.

"That one has always kept to himself. I heard they wouldn't even give him a room here when he was workin' on the gardens. The hotel wasn't even open yet. I mean, yeah he's a Japanese and all, but you would think..." Leticia said.

Penelope nodded with agreement that it was a slight. No wonder he was so resentful during the event. Still, she had a feeling his dour mood was more than a reaction to simple prejudice. What had Genevieve said to him prior to his speech? What is it he wanted from Gary? And what had Bentley wanted with him?

Then there was the wife of that golfer. What was going on there?

She put those thoughts aside in favor of more funny tales about the hotel's first guests this week. Apparently, the golfer who had made such a scene earlier was Robert Lee Paxton, a famous player who was in town for a high-stakes tournament. He was well-liked among the staff, mostly for being personable and good for a laugh. But they were clueless about his wife, Betty who had been strangely quiet and kept to herself all week.

They were interrupted when a pretty young woman with copper ringlets and dimples for days popped in. Underneath the light jacket, she had on slightly parted, Pen could see the same black uniform with a white apron that the other maids wore. The jacket didn't do much to disguise the same shapely figure the other maids also had. She flashed those green eyes around the room, causing a stir, then settled them on Gary.

"Hiya Gary," she said with a coy smile.

"Hey, doll," he said with a grin.

She leaned in and whispered in his ear. Based on his suddenly thoughtful expression, it wasn't words of sweet nothing. He sighed, then nodded. She pulled away, grinning prettily before popping back out.

"I gotta blouse for a minute. You want to call it quits or keep going?" He asked Penelope. "I shouldn't be too long."

"If you think I'm not going home with all the kale, you're sorely mistaken."

He chuckled and reached down to gather up his winnings. "In which case, I should probably take this with me."

"You don't trust us, or something?" Thomas said, mostly teasing.

"Not a bit," Gary said with a laugh. He turned to Penelope. "I'll be back in two shakes."

Penelope was fine waiting, mostly because the staff was still happy to oblige her sinful taste for gossip. They had moved on to the other notorious guests of the hotel.

"And that Bentley Green? He and that young thing with him booked the Honeymoon Suite if you can believe it," Leticia continued.

"Is she even old enough to get married?" Rosie asked with a guilty grin.

"One would have thought he'd at least pick the Bridal Suite, which is still available. But that would have probably given his little tart ideas he had no interest in entertaining," Leticia said.

"He lives in New York, though. Why would he stay here?" Penelope asked.

The maids laughed and gave her knowing looks.

"Why does any man book a hotel with a cute young thing?"

Penelope left that alone but still found it perplexing. Yes, men liked to flaunt their conquests, but usually not to such an ostentatious degree. He could just as easily have his bit of fun with Darlene in his Upper East Side townhome, away from judgmental eyes. To not only stay in a hotel that was currently the talk of the town, but book the Honeymoon Suite on top of that?

Strange.

"At any rate, my shift has long been over," Rosie said, pulling herself up. "I need to get outta this thing and into some regular clothes."

Those words and the cat-like stretch she gave had every eye settled on her, even Pen's. While not *quite* as voluptuous as the lovely Mandy was, she was enough to make Penelope wonder if perhaps this hotel had a preferential type when it came to maids. In an era where most women took pains to flatten their chests and practically starve themselves thin, the maids at this hotel seemed to embrace their womanly curves.

Leticia stayed, her shift apparently not over. They continued chatting about the hotel and what it was like to work there as well as its interesting guests.

"Do you think Gary got lost?" Penelope asked after quite a bit of time had passed. "Or maybe just a little... distracted by a certain maid?"

Leticia laughed. "Rosie maybe, though he treats her like a kid sister, much to her disappointment. As for that Mandy? He *definitely* ain't her kind of man."

The knowing looks that circulated around the room created a ripple of controversy in the air. Before Penelope was bold enough to finally ask, there was commotion coming from the hallway outside. Everyone's attention was diverted to the door, waiting to see what was astir.

Wendell Dickens burst through, looking frazzled.

"Everyone—" He stopped short when he saw Penelope. A look of panic struck his face but quickly transformed into irritation. "What's the meaning of this? *What* is going on here?"

The staff all took on guilty looks and turned to Penelope to explain herself.

"I seem to have gotten lost," she said in a cheery tone.

Wendell eyed the glass in her hand, the cards, and the money in front of her place at the table then narrowed his gaze.

"Please come with me, ma'am," he said in a clipped voice.

Penelope sighed, and brazenly finished what was left in her glass. No sense in it going to waste. She collected her money, stood up, and followed Mr. Dickens into the hallway, which was even more crowded with staff than before.

Any air of deferential treatment was lost as Wendell gestured for Penelope to go ahead of him. When she seemed to be taking her time, he gently took her arm and hurried her along.

"I beg your pardon," she scoffed.

"You should not be down here, ma'am."

"It's Penelope Banks, and as I said, I took a wrong turn—"

"Please don't insult my intelligence with lies."

"Then perhaps you can tell me the meaning of this, Mr. Dickens? Is it about Gary?" Perhaps this was why he had been taking so long. "If he's in any trouble, I can assure you that the fault lies entirely with me."

He stopped and studied her. "What do you know about Gary?"

It was such a vague question, that she didn't dare answer. Obviously something more serious than the staff getting caught with the clientele was at hand.

"What's this about?" she repeated.

"There's been an...incident."

"Is Gary alright?" Pen asked with concern.

"How, may I ask, is Gary any of your concern?" Again he studied her.

"He's a...friend of mine. Now tell me what is going on."

Mr. Dickens paused before answering, then steeled his gaze.

"Your *friend*, Gary has murdered Jiro Ishida."

CHAPTER FOUR

Penelope sat in one of the chairs in the lobby of the Grand Opal Hotel. She stared out numbly at the buzz of activity around her. Members of the staff huddled in groups, staring around with wide, worried eyes. Policemen in uniform hovered nearby, making sure that no one left, and also keeping any outsiders at bay.

It was a muddled atmosphere that clashed horribly with the beautifully serene interior. The design of the lobby had followed modern minimalist trends, with clean lines and a light, open feel. Huge Japanese lanterns hanging from the ceiling cast a warm glow against the comfortable, straight-lined sofas and chairs. The cream rugs underneath had patterns of bamboo. Rectangular tables with low, round vases held white orchids. A large table near the front door held a giant vase filled with cherry blossom branches in full bloom.

Through the front doors, Penelope could already see members of the press eagerly hoping to learn more about what had happened tonight.

Penelope was just as curious.

Jiro Ishida was dead?

Killed by Gary?

What in the world had happened in the forty minutes he'd been gone? What had Mandy whispered in his ear? What did any of it have to do with Mr. Ishida?

As a self-employed private investigator, Penelope was already working through how something like this could have happened. More importantly, how it could have been committed by Gary of all people. She didn't know him all that well, but she liked to consider herself a good judge of character, and she really liked him. He may have been a hustler, but he didn't seem like the murdering type.

Then again, sometimes desperation or panic made people commit the worst kinds of evil.

He obviously had a side business dealing with black market goods, which meant he was cozy with unsavory types. Frankly, the same could be said of herself. It didn't mean he was any more a murderer than Pen was.

Perhaps it had to do with what he had briefly discussed with Jiro during the party? What had Jiro been requesting of him?

The police were corralling the staff, at least those who weren't senior, into a separate area. This late at night, the few guests would have been in their suites. Penelope could understand not knocking on their door under the guise of questioning them, at least not right away.

However, she wasn't the only guest from the party there in the lobby.

Robert Paxton and Bentley Green were both in one of the seating area vignettes, quietly arguing with one another. Or at least Robert was arguing with Bentley. He was quite obviously zozzled, nearly falling out of his chair as he leaned in towards the more sedate Bentley. Upon closer inspection, the latter actually looked quite angered, insulted even, as he stared back at the far more animated Robert.

Finally, Bentley shot up from his chair and leaned in to hiss something at Robert that had him shutting up. Then, Bentley stormed away to one of the detectives and argued with him.

Robert stared after him, seemingly confused. He caught Penelope staring at him and a lopsided grin came to his face. Pen waited too long to turn away and he took that as an invitation to pull himself up and stagger over. He fell onto the sofa to the left of her chair, his right arm settled on the armrest, and legs spread wide, the right knee only inches from hers.

"I hope that little argument wasn't too upsetting for you, ma'am. I sometimes use colorful language when I'm in my cups."

"I didn't hear a thing," Penelope assured him, hoping he'd go away.

He seemed to relax with relief and settled back on the couch, much to her annoyance.

"It seems that Japanese went and got himself into trouble."

"He was *murdered*," she corrected.

"Right, right," he said thoughtfully, his gaze sharpened as he studied her. "I recognize you from the party, don't I? I never forget a gorgeous face."

"Yes, I was there," she said noncommittally, hoping he'd take the hint and leave her to her thoughts.

"Hard to miss in that pretty dress of yours. And those bright blue eyes? Any red-blooded man could spot those a mile away."

He wasn't just zozzled, he was flirting. With his outrageous sense of humor and charm, not to mention being a famous golfer, he was probably used to most women responding favorably to it. Penelope had no interest.

It wasn't that he was unattractive. He looked to be in his thirties but still had boyish good looks that probably allowed more people to give him a pass when he acted like an ass. Which he was very much doing at this moment.

Still, she did wonder why he was down here in the lobby with her. Without his wife.

And what *was* that argument with Bentley Green about?

"Robert Lee Paxton is the name. Named after the good general himself, but most of my friends call me Bobby."

"Penelope Banks." She didn't bother stating that most of her friends called her Pen. She had no intention of becoming *that* familiar with this man, thus giving him ideas. "Were you out touring the city tonight?"

He grinned, looking like the cat that ate the canary. "You could, ah, say that."

"I presume it wasn't the Statue of Liberty you were visiting," she said dryly.

He barked out a laugh so loud it made Penelope cringe. Understandably, several policemen looked their way with frowns on their faces.

"You got a sense of humor on you. I like that in a woman."

"Is that what attracted you to your *wife*? Betty, I believe you said her name was," she hinted.

He assessed her and a slow smile spread across his face.

"Ahh." He pulled himself up, grimacing a bit as he did, which revealed just how ossified he was. He leaned in closer to her and winked. Penelope could smell the alcohol on him. "Not to worry, darlin', I know what line not to cross with the fairer sex."

He lifted his left hand and used his thumb to fiddle with the ring on it for her benefit.

"I take it you were touring some of our city's more *notorious* establishments."

He chuckled. "And what a visit it was, my dear. I tell ya, down in Georgia we got our own, uh, *establishments* where a man can wet his whistle just fine. They have their own kind of charm, or lack thereof depending on how deep into the backwoods you want to go. But y'all Yanks...?" He grinned and shook his head in wonder. "Let's just say I had a mighty swell time of it."

"Apparently." She studied him. "But I remember you bragging about bringing some of your own homebrew with you."

His gaze narrowed slightly with suspicion but quickly relaxed again. "I can drink that stuff any ole time I want. Tonight I was looking for something...different."

I'm sure, Penelope thought to herself.

"How did you even know where such a place was, let alone how to get in?"

Most speakeasies were discovered via word of mouth and required a password, invitation, or membership to get in. It didn't surprise Penelope that this man would be able to obtain such information, she just wondered how.

He touched the side of his nose and winked again. "I have my sources. One thing I can say about Betty is that she picked the right hotel this time around. The staff here certainly knows how to accommodate," he said with a grin. It faded as he thought of something. His eyes flashed to Bentley and narrowed with anger. "At least most of the time."

"Was it Gary who told you about the place you went tonight?"

His eyes shot right back to her, wide with surprise. "How'd you know that?"

"He seems to be the fellow who can—how'd you put it? —accommodate."

He shot her an *aw-shucks* grin. "What can I say? A man has needs."

"He's also the fellow accused of killing Jiro Ishida."

"You don't say?" he exclaimed, looking thoroughly stunned. His brow furrowed with dismay. "Well damn, what in the Sam Hill did he go and do that for?"

"I don't think he did it. Do you?"

His eyes darted back to her, surprisingly lucid now. "I wouldn't know, would I?" He said in an even, slightly defensive voice.

"Did you *just* get back from your night out?"

He was silent for once, assessing her in quiet contemplation. "I think I'd better go and see what's the hold up in gettin' back to my suite."

With that, he was overly careful as he struggled to his feet, obviously aware of how drunk he was, especially in front of the police. Hopefully, whatever golf tournament he was here to play in New York wasn't tomorrow. She didn't imagine playing with a body still recovering from a hangover would do him any favors. Then again, maybe he was one of those athletes that performed better while under the influence.

Either way, her little interrogation was over. She watched him strut over to one of the policemen, full of swagger and booze. He grabbed the nearest officer and began protesting. The officer gently led Bobby away.

Penelope relaxed and thought over the brief discussion. Bobby obviously knew Gary in more than just a waiter-guest capacity. He also knew Jiro—more to the point, his wife, Betty, did. Quite intimately, at least based on the way they interacted during the party.

That certainly spelled motive.

The question was when had Bobby Lee returned from his night at the nearest speakeasy? If he had even been at one in the first place.

These thoughts were instantly wrenched from her mind by the commotion coming from the main elevators.

"I swear, it wasn't me!"

Penelope sat up straighter as she saw two police officers sandwiched on either side of Gary, now in handcuffs. He was wet for some reason, the cuffs of his shirt rolled up to reveal his cut arm, but still dripping water on the floor. The officers were escorting him toward the exit, despite his protests. He looked around, panic on his face. His eyes landed on Penelope and widened.

"Miss Banks! You have to help me. I didn't kill him, I swear! You said you worked on stuff like this. Please, I'll do anything, just—"

He was out the front door before he could finish the rest. Penelope felt her sympathy kick in. She had set up her little investigative business in the first place to help those most likely to need it. It seemed Gary, despite all his connections, had found himself in just such a situation. If he was being set up as a scapegoat for this, or even just a guy caught in the wrong place at the wrong time, she absolutely planned on helping him.

"Why am I not surprised to find you here, Miss Banks?"

Penelope started in surprise at that familiar voice. She twisted around in her chair to confront the man attached to it, eyes widening when they confirmed who it was.

He stared down at her from between full, dark lashes that always made her sigh internally. His handsome face, dark eyes, sharp nose, and hard jaw could grace a movie screen. The only flaw was the burn scar, a memento from the Great War. It covered the lower part of his right jaw below the ear and down the neck. It was barely noticeable as he faced Penelope head-first, but even with a full view of it, she found it oddly endearing, though he had yet to tell her in detail how he got it.

"Detective Prescott?"

CHAPTER FIVE

Detective Richard Prescott stared down at Penelope with the usual look of surprise and consternation he wore whenever the two of them ran into one another. In all fairness, their interactions thus far had mostly been when Penelope was involved with a case, or as he liked to put it, meddling in police affairs.

Now that Penelope thought on it, the Grand Opal Hotel fell just within the jurisdiction of the 10A precinct. How wonderfully convenient for her.

He sighed and the barest hint of a cynical smile touched his mouth. "It seems you've somehow managed to entangle yourself in a murder case yet again."

Penelope shot up from her chair. "Are you working this murder? What happened? How did Mr. Ishida die? Do you think it was intentional or just an accident? Where did it—"

"Miss Banks," he said, holding up a hand to silence her. "We seem to have a fundamental misunderstanding about *who* is the detective here."

"Of course," she said, giving him a demure look that he

didn't believe for one second. "By all means, ask me any questions you have, detective."

Hopefully during his interrogation, she could glean more information about exactly what had happened.

"I don't think it would be prudent that I be the one to question you, considering our history together."

"Our history?" she repeated in a teasing tone.

"You know what I mean. It would be unprofessional. There's an obvious conflict of interest."

"Why?" She smiled and batted her eyelashes. "I'd be far more forthcoming with you than I would any other detective."

"Those aren't exactly the words of an innocent person."

"Am I a suspect?" she asked, incredulous. That would mean they had doubts about Gary.

He paused, then conceded, "No. But you have suddenly become a person of interest."

"Because I was with the man you arrested just prior to him *supposedly* committing murder?"

"Were you?" he asked, his jaw tightening, eyes darkening.

Penelope smiled and studied him speculatively. "Just how much do you know?"

"Once again, I think you have our roles reversed. *I* should be asking how much *you* know."

"Quite a bit, as it turns out."

His brow rose. "Is that so?"

"I was at the party earlier, and noticed several very suspicions things."

"My understanding is that the party ended several hours ago. What were you doing in the meantime?"

"As I said, I was with your suspect just before the

murder took place. If you'd like to know more about that, I suppose you'll just have to question me."

She pursed her lips with pleasure.

He tightened his with displeasure.

Penelope waited for him to come to his senses. Finally, he sighed and sat on the sofa, the same spot Bobby Lee had vacated only moments ago. Though he wasn't barbaric enough to spread his legs as widely, Penelope didn't mind the proximity of his knee to her stockinged leg as she took her seat again.

"What is it you know, Miss Banks?"

"I can say that Jiro Ishida wasn't at all happy tonight. I suspect there might be some animosity between him and the owner of this hotel, Genevieve Walton. Perhaps a dispute over payment? You'd have to ask her, or her manager Wendell Dickens."

Detective Prescott nodded, as though saving that bit of information to address later when he questioned Wendell Dickens and Genevieve Walton, which Penelope hoped he would be thorough enough to do.

"Also, that Robert Lee Paxton—Bobby to his friends—the one your officers handled a moment ago? He may very well have motive, perhaps even opportunity. He just informed me that he was *supposedly* out exploring one of the various tourist attractions that New York has to offer. The kind that is, *ahem*, very much *prohibited*?"

"I see," Detective Prescott said with a wry smile. Penelope knew him to be more tolerant than any officer of the law should be, at least when it came to private citizens and illegal drinking. Though, as far as she knew, he never broke the law himself.

"But who knows where he really was? His wife, Betty, seemed awfully cozy with Mr. Ishida during the party. If I didn't know any better, I'd suspect something indelicate. I doubt Mr. Paxton is the kind who would take too kindly to his wife having an extramarital relationship, he seems rather excitable. Especially in his condition."

"Drunk?"

"Very. He also knew Gary."

"Gary is it?" He arched an eyebrow at her use of his familiar name.

"Mr. Garret," she said primly.

"It seems you also know the suspect...quite well," he remarked in a tight voice.

"And for good reason. Gary is, how shall I put it, the kind of man who can procure things?"

"Such as?"

"A very good bottle of Macallan? A good game of poker with decent stakes?"

His brow furrowed. "I'm going to pretend you're speaking academically."

"That's probably for the best. All the same, it works out for our purposes."

"Our?"

"You don't honestly think I'd let you send an innocent man to prison, do you?"

"You're so sure he's innocent?"

"You're so sure he isn't?"

Detective Prescott studied her, his expression revealing that he knew exactly what she was doing. Finally he sighed.

"He was found up in the gardens on the roof, not only with blood on him but with Jiro Ishida's body in his hands."

Penelope blinked in surprise at that. "How did he die?"

"There was an injury on his head which could have been the cause. But Mr. Ishida was also mostly wet. They were found right by the koi pond, and it looks like Mr.

Garret had drowned him. We'll have to wait for the coroner to make a definitive call."

Penelope absorbed that, tempering down the bile she felt rise at imagining poor Jiro Ishida's death. To die in such a way, and on a night that celebrated one of his crowning achievements. The gardens upstairs, as beautiful as they were, would have made him one of the most sought-after garden designers on the East Coast if not the country.

"Who found them?"

"The manager of the hotel, Mr. Dickens. He claims a guest in one of the top-level suites heard some commotion above them and he went to check."

"I see," Penelope said in thought.

But what was Gary doing up there? Now she *really* wanted to know what Mandy had said to him.

Detective Prescott cleared his throat, catching her attention again. "You mentioned you noticed *several* suspicious things during the party? Was there anything else?"

"Right," Penelope said, straightening and focusing again. "Bentley Green was there, supposedly conducting business. He's an—"

"Architect, yes, I know of him."

Penelope smiled, once again marveling at how informed her favorite detective was. Also at what a mystery he was. From the few months she had known him, ever since he'd come to work on the case in Long Island that involved Agnes Sterling, she'd learned that he had gone to Princeton University, had a thorough knowledge of art, and had served in the Great War, most likely as a pilot, but even that much was ambiguous.

"You're familiar with him and his work?"

"Just because I'm a detective, doesn't mean I'm an uncultured boor, Miss Banks."

"I certainly didn't mean to imply that."

"Of course, but you were saying...?"

"Yes, well, he mentioned something about conducting business while at the party. He had a brief word with Mr. Ishida, who didn't seem all that inclined to indulge him based on the looks of things. He had earlier told his date—his rather *young* date—that fairly soon she'd have access to another garden filled with bonsai trees for her to enjoy. Nothing suspicious in and of itself, but I've learned that when it comes to business, men can be fairly cutthroat. So to speak."

Though she did manage to get a tiny smile out of him, Detective Prescott didn't seem too impressed by this bit of knowledge. Still, she knew him to be a fair and thorough detective, so he'd at least ask Bentley about his business tonight.

"Is that all?"

Penelope mentally reversed back to the events of the night. There was that strange man who seemed upset at the *plebeian* masses being exposed to something as cultured as Japanese gardens, but that was hardly motive for murder. She didn't want Detective Prescott wasting his time with people whose only sin was being a snob.

"You should check with a maid named Mandy, she was the one to send Gary up to the roof in the first place I think. At the very least, she got him out of the staff area where I was just about to murder him—figuratively speaking," Penelope added with a smile when she saw the look on his face. "At poker."

"I see. Mandy, you said her name was?"

"Yes."

"So, you were in the staff area playing cards at the time of the murder?"

"As many members of the staff and the band from tonight can attest to. Sorry to disappoint you, I know how much you enjoy it when I'm a suspect."

He tightened his lips to keep from smiling. "Anything else you can remember?"

Penelope thought about Sam from the band. He wasn't too happy about losing all of his money, and he'd been gone for a while by the time Wendell came down and escorted her away.

Still, she kept that to herself. She certainly didn't suspect Detective Prescott of being prejudiced—thus far, he'd shown an admirable degree of open-mindedness about many things—but she didn't want any of his fellow members of the force to catch the scent. Once there was a whiff of suspicion cast on a colored man, many of them would be champing at the bit to slap the handcuffs on him.

All the better for her to do a bit of private detecting on her own.

"Not that I can think of. But I'll be sure to let you know if I learn anything."

"That sounds an awful lot like you intend to meddle in this investigation."

"Nonsense, when have I ever meddled?"

He gave her a deadpan look in response to that.

"Okay, but has it not always worked in your favor?"

"Miss Banks," he sighed.

"I've given you plenty of people to question, Detective Prescott. I certainly don't want the police department's resources wasted on nonsense that probably doesn't amount to anything."

"Such as?"

"Such as information that, say, a guest of the hotel could pick up in passing?"

"Would that guest happen to be you?" he asked in a clipped and very disapproving tone.

"Funny you should ask. I was just telling myself that I was so impressed with the gardens upstairs, I *had* to see what the rooms were like as well."

"Should I even bother cautioning you, *yet again*, about interfering in a police investigation?"

"I could recite it from memory by now, detective," she said with a pert smile.

"Yes, I know," he said dryly. "And yet it never seems to take hold."

"Is my interrogation over? I'd like to book my room before they are all taken."

"Something tells me you might not have a problem. Murder is usually bad for business."

Unless that business was private detecting. And as far as Penelope was concerned, that business was now in high demand.

CHAPTER SIX

Once Detective Prescott was done questioning her, making sure to leave her with yet another caution against meddling, Penelope made her way to the front desk at the Grand Opal Hotel.

Or at least she tried to.

"I'm afraid the rest of the hotel is off-limits, ma'am," said a policeman blocking her way.

"I'm a guest," she lied. "I just need to request something from the front desk, before returning to my room."

He seemed uncertain as to whether he should let her through or instruct her to go straight to her room, which would have been problematic, seeing as she didn't really have one.

"Surely you saw me being questioned by Detective Prescott just now? He's cleared me." She feigned a distraught look. "Honestly, this whole business of murder has me so upset, I think I might faint at any moment. All I wanted was a simple reassurance from the front desk that a rather delicate matter—a *feminine* matter—would be handled and put me at ease. But now, I'm being manhandled by the police and—"

"Please, please, ma'am, just calm down." The crease above his widened eyes betrayed the turmoil going on in his head.

Penelope felt *slightly* bad. She'd used the most powerful arsenal in every woman's armory—tears and the mention of anything intimately feminine. Still, she couldn't help it if it always worked on men. Perhaps this would be a signal that they should hire more female police officers; not a single one of them would have bought her act.

"I suppose it's fine to let you go to the front desk, but *only* to the front desk."

"Oh, thank you ever so much. You truly are a gentleman," she gushed, rewarding him with a flattering smile that made him have to clear his throat.

The young man at the front desk met Penelope with a professional smile that couldn't quite conceal his wariness. He was probably steeling himself for the onslaught of questions and protests from the Grand Opal's guests.

"Good evening ma'am, how can I help you?"

"I'm Penelope Banks, one of the guests from the party. I was so impressed with everything, I'd like a room."

"You...you want to *reserve* a room?" His confusion was understandable considering the circumstances. Despite her complimentary words about the party and gardens, it was impossible to miss the police presence in the lobby.

"Actually, I'd like a room for *tonight*, if one is available."

"I-um..." His brow furrowed with dismay and even more confusion. He looked around for help and seemed to catch the eye of someone behind her. "I need to, ah, see if one is available. Please give me a moment."

Penelope frowned as he walked away. True, they

weren't officially open, but surely they had made allowances for people from the party wanting a room for the night, especially after several weeks of grand announcements in the paper. Surely the information he needed was right here at the front desk.

She turned to see where he had gone and felt her frustration set in when she saw him approach the hotel manager. She could sniff the obstruction wafting from Wendell Dickens even at a distance. Sure enough, when the front desk man gestured in her direction, Wendell's eyes met hers and narrowed with suspicion.

After all, what guest with any pure motives would book a room at a hotel where they'd just learned a murder had taken place?

He plastered a fake smile on his face and walked over, the young man from the front desk scurrying after him.

"Miss Banks, is it? I'm afraid what rooms we have available are fully booked for tonight. As you know, we don't officially open until tomorrow, and as such most of the rooms are not quite ready. I encourage you to reserve one of those rooms now though because—"

"Odd, because I had it on good authority that the Bridal Suite was available."

"The Bridal Suite?" He eyed her, wondering if there was a reason she had chosen that particular room.

In truth, it was the only one she knew was vacant and available to book, based on what Leticia had said. Now, she was glad that particular suite had been mentioned, she was already devising how it could work in her favor.

"I'm afraid even that one isn't available."

Of course he would say that. He could probably sense the meddlesome nature radiating from Penelope even before he caught her playing cards with the staff. The last thing any hotel manager wanted was someone sniffing around, especially when a murder had just taken place in the newly opened hotel.

But Penelope had never been that easily dissuaded from anything. She thought of several ways to go about this. Playing the bully rarely worked with officious men such as Wendell Dickens, at least not when you were a woman. On that note, he was hardly likely to be moved by any feminine wiles or playing the wilting violet, not after the compromising circumstances he'd caught her in.

She chose the third option.

"Pineapples!" she said, biting her lip in frustration. "And to think, my only purpose for coming tonight was to tell all my female friends and acquaintances at the Young Ladies' Historical Preservation Society what a perfect venue this hotel would be for their weddings."

The name of that organization lit a fire in his eyes. Never mind that Penelope wasn't exactly a member of the Society. In fact, after a recent murder—one which she had helped solve, thank you very much!—it had been not so gently suggested that she never attend one of their meetings again.

It seemed no good deed went unpunished.

All the same, at twenty-four, she was of the right age. More importantly, if she had been able to purchase a ticket for the party, she was certainly in the right social circles. It was enough to make her suggestion believable. All the same, it didn't hurt to add a little cream to coffee just to make sure.

"So many of the members are recently engaged you see, and each of them is *clamoring* for something unique and modern as a venue. The Ritz, the Astor, and the Plaza are so passé, you know. I absolutely fell in love with the gardens and thought I might be able to tell them how positively *divine* the Bridal Suite was as well. Certainly, my glowing review would have been something to overshadow this *ghastly* news of murder that's certain to be splashed over the front pages of the newspapers in the coming weeks." She gave him a demure but pointed look. "I suppose I'll have to tell them that the murder *apparently* had something to do with the Bridal Suite. Is that why it isn't available? You know how superstitious brides are about these things."

Wendell had a set look on his face, but Penelope could see the panic in his eyes. "I think perhaps we can accommodate you, after all, Miss Banks."

"Oh, how wonderful!" she exclaimed, clasping her hands together in appreciation.

"The rate will be five hundred dollars a night."

An obscene amount, but for one of the very best suites in one of the finest, newest hotels in New York City, it was understandable. If he had been hoping that would dissuade Penelope, he was sorely mistaken.

"Very well," she said pertly. "I'll have the money wired first thing in the morning."

To his credit, Wendell's sigh of resignation was barely noticeable.

"I must insist that you remain only in the *guest* areas," he warned in a terse voice. "In fact, until the, ah, matters with the police are complete, guests are limited only to their rooms and the Lotus Blossom Restaurant when it opens during mealtimes of course. There is, however, room service available at any hour."

Penelope smiled accommodatingly.

"Do you have any luggage for one of our bellmen to take to your room?" he asked in a sardonic tone.

"I'm having it delivered in the morning." An easy enough task.

"Of course," Wendell said flatly. "In which case, welcome to the Grand Opal Hotel, Miss Banks, I hope you enjoy your stay. I'll have Stanley show you up to your room."

He caught the attention of one of the bellhops who was lingering in the lobby, seemingly thrilled at the late-night excitement. His brow rose in mild surprise when he realized he was being called to escort a new guest to her room.

"Stanley, please escort Miss Banks to the Bridal Suite on the sixteenth floor," Wendell said, handing him a gold key with an intricately braided attachment done in thin, white, silk rope, with a tassel at the end.

"Yes, sir," Stanley said, stopping just short of saluting. He grinned at Penelope. "Please follow me, ma'am."

She followed him to the elevator, assessing just how much she could pry out of him before they reached her floor. The Grand Opal Hotel had seventeen floors, not quite as many as the Plaza nearby, but still practically a skyscraper by 5th Avenue standards. The way new development was going in Manhattan, it might very well be dwarfed within a decade or so. That gave them at least a few minutes before they reached the sixteenth floor.

And Penelope had learned early on the best lubricant to loosen lips. Once they were ensconced in the privacy of the elevator, she readied herself to apply it.

"Quite a buzz of activity going on tonight, isn't it?"

"Yes, ma'am," Stanley said with a professional smile.

"I can't imagine why anyone would want to kill Mr. Ishida, can you?"

"No ma'am," he said, just as tactfully.

"Anything you care to tell me about what might have

been going on with Mr. Ishida tonight? He seemed quite unhappy considering the party was in his honor."

Stanley grinned and gave her a sly look. "I might..."

Penelope smirked. "The boy knows how to make a buck, I can appreciate that."

She opened her purse and pulled out a five-dollar bill, dangling it before him. It was absurdly more than the usual tip a bellhop received, even if he was carting luggage. But information was an expensive commodity.

"This better be worth it."

Stanley plucked the bill from her hand. "That's for you to decide ma'am."

"What have you got?"

"I do know that this hotel...? Well, I heard Miss Walton poured every penny she had into it, and when I say every, I do mean down to the last nickel. I don't know nothin' about those Japanese, but I'd say it turned out pretty swanky. Apparently, there were some big ticket items bought specifically for that garden up top. Anyway, the long and short of it is, there maybe wasn't enough to cover everything when all was said and done."

"Such as?"

"Such as maybe that Mr. Ishida didn't get paid."

That would certainly make anyone a bit cantankerous. No wonder he was so angry at the party.

"What else have you heard?"

"Mostly noise. I'm thinking Miss Walton probably thought she could get away with it, him being Japanese and all."

"So Jiro Ishida didn't insist on being paid upfront?"

Stanley just shrugged, though they both knew the answer to that.

"Is there anything else you can tell me?"

"What is it you'd like to know? There's a lot that goes on in a hotel."

"I really just want to find out if Gary really might have killed him. What reason would he have to do such a thing?"

One side of Stanley's mouth hitched up and he coughed out a sharp laugh. "Gary has friends, he'll be fine."

"Friends?"

He gave her a cynical look. "Friends like you."

In other words, wealthy.

"Right, what about enemies?"

"Aim too high and that's what you get, I say. See me? I stick to tips, like the very generous one you offered—thanks by the way. I don't try to make friends. Gary, he liked to rub shoulders, sometimes with people who know how to make enemies. It doesn't surprise me that he got hit with the buckshot."

"So Mr. Ishida was a 'friend' of his?"

"It wouldn't surprise me."

The elevator came to a stop on the sixteenth floor and the doors opened. That seemed to flip a switch which had him shutting up.

"After you, ma'am."

Penelope sighed and exited the elevator into a very nice hallway with lush carpeting and silk-covered walls done in a similar bamboo pattern as the rugs downstairs. There were only three doors on this floor, one directly ahead and one at either end of the hallway. The one directly ahead was labeled the "Oriental Suite."

Stanley walked ahead of her, leading her to the door at the end of the hall to their left.

"I suppose the Emperor Suite is above us?" Penelope asked.

"Along with the Presidential Suite."

That was something different. Penelope remembered the days when the higher floors were the least desirable, reserved for staff. With electricity powering almost everything these days, elevators and electric fans had made the top-level floors tolerable. When combined with the more subdued noise of traffic, privacy, and the views, they had become preferable these days.

"The Bridal Suite," he announced with flair as he unlocked and opened the door for her.

Penelope was too momentarily awestruck as she walked in to continue her interrogation.

"Your key, ma'am," Stanley said, catching her attention.

She tore her eyes away from the interior—she had the rest of the night to explore its wonders—and dragged them back to the bellhop.

"Can you think of any reason why *anyone* would want to kill Jiro Ishida?" she asked point-blank.

He sighed, and closed the door. "All's I know is while he was up there finishing up that garden this week, there were a few members of the staff that liked to be up there as well. Including a certain maid."

Well, well, well...

"Any maid in particular?" Penelope urged.

He just worked his jaw as though that was a confidence too many.

"Mandy, perhaps?"

He tried to remain neutral but Penelope had learned to read a poker face, and the way the muscle in his lower left jaw feathered told her everything.

"I don't suppose she's working tonight?"

"She's still here. Her shift doesn't end until morning."

"I don't suppose it's too late for turn down service is it?" She hinted. Pen reached into her purse for another five dollars. "This is for you if you can get her up here. Tell her there's just as much of this for her if she does."

He seemed hesitant.

"If you're worried about her learning you told me anything, she won't. She'll assume it's based on my previous encounter with her."

He gave her a curious look, and she knew he was itching to ask what that was about. It's no wonder he knew so much; he had the same curious—or meddlesome—mind she did.

"Thank you, Stanley," she said with a pointed smile.

"Yes, ma'am. I'll make sure Mandy is available," he said, taking the final five dollars and leaving.

When he left she exhaled in exasperation.

"Zounds, this case is going to cost me," Penelope said, remembering the rate of the room.

But she was worth so much, it hardly behooved her to complain. According to her attorney, Mr. Wilcox, who also handled overseeing her financial affairs, she would recoup the cost of the room by the time she woke up in the morning. All without lifting a finger. Even though she'd grown up with a father who made his fortune working on Wall Street, it still boggled her mind that people made so much money doing positively nothing.

Still, she was here now so she might as well enjoy it. Penelope turned her attention back to the room and once again fell into awe.

"Let's discover what five hundred dollars a night gets you," she said, perfectly mesmerized.

CHAPTER SEVEN

The foyer where Penelope dropped her purse and her key was paneled in dark wood and had white marble flooring. A small, round, flat vase on the console table held a white orchid plant. An oval mirror above it reflected the awe in her gaze before she turned it to the rest of the suite.

Pen slipped out of her shoes and explored. The sitting area occupied a corner so there were large picture-window views of Central Park on one side and lower Manhattan on the other. That was another benefit of being so high up. This floor towered over most other buildings so Penelope could see quite a distance.

The furniture—a large circular couch and two armchairs—was done in a cream fabric. It matched the color scheme of the room including the pearlescent white papered walls. The coffee table and sitting table near the window were in the same dark wood as the entryway. On almost every surface Penelope saw a wide vase of white orchids.

There was a bar, but Pen was too jaded to believe that it held anything other than accoutrements for the beautiful white tea service that sat atop it, complete with an electric heater.

Against one wall was a desk with fine stationery atop a blotter, complete with a nice ink pen, and a lovely letter opener, the handle of which was inlaid with mother-of-pearl and had the hotel logo etched into it.

She ignored that in favor of exploring the bedroom. There were two doors on either side of the large sitting area so she chose the one that led to a room offering a view of Central Park, assuming it was the main one.

She gasped with delight as she opened it. Everything was white and cream again, including the large bed with a total of eight pillows. What really drew her attention was the beautiful mural of cherry blossom trees, pink flowers in full bloom, above the bed. In an armoire she found a lovely kimono in white with pink cherry blossoms, matching the mural.

Penelope wasn't the overly feminine or sentimental type—not after having her fairytale romantic notions dashed by a cheating fiancé—but she couldn't help the small swoon that came to her. It really was a room fit for a princess, one who was soon to become a queen.

She wandered into the spacious bathroom, also done in white. There was a clawfoot tub as a central focus, almost large enough to swim in. On the vanity that held two sinks, she saw several bottles and vials, no doubt various oils, lotions, and other toiletries. Two large fluffy towels hung from a rack next to it.

Pen went back into the bedroom and fell onto the bed, sinking into the soft, lush comfort of it. The white curtains had been drawn open to reveal Central Park. A few blocks north, Penelope had her own view of the park from her apartment, but it wasn't quite this high. From here, she really did feel like a queen looking out over her realm.

Whatever money Genevieve had sunk into this hotel it had been worth it, at least in terms of the result. It was, of course, sad it had come at the expense of payment for services rendered to Jiro Ishida.

As though on cue, Penelope heard a knock at the door.

She scooted to the edge of the bed and stood up to go answer it. Pen was pleased to see Mandy standing in the hallway, dimples on full display.

That wasn't all that was on display. With her jacket now off, Pen had a much better view of her maid's uniform. It was practically a second skin, clinging to each and every curve of hers. It was also exceptionally short, falling at least a few inches above the knees. Darlene's hemline from the party had been brow-raising, but this one was heart-racing. If it wasn't for the opaque stockings she wore, it would be scandalous.

"You asked for your bed to be turned down?" Mandy asked with a perfectly innocent look. She had brought her cart up with her, perhaps a requirement of her duties.

"Yes, please," Penelope said in a diplomatic tone, just in case anyone in the other suites was listening. She opened the door wider for the maid to enter.

"I've also brought up fresh supplies, towels and such. There was no time to ready the suite before you reserved it."

"Yes, yes, that's fine."

Mandy walked in quickly enough, pushing the cart ahead of her. She slowed down once she entered the room as though she too was enthralled by it.

"It's beautiful isn't it?" Penelope said behind her.

Mandy started, as though pulled out of a daze. She

turned to give Penelope an apologetic smile. "I'll start with the guest room first. I assume you're in the bridal bedroom?"

"I am."

"Very good, ma'am."

Penelope watched Mandy push the cart into the guest bedroom but stayed behind. She didn't want to hover, pestering her while she did her job. At least in the bridal bedroom, it wouldn't seem out of place for her to be in the same room. This gave her time to think about the best approach to questioning her.

When Mandy came back out, she flashed a quick smile at Pen who stood further on by her bedroom door. Mandy parked her cart near the entryway and reached underneath the dark cloth that masked the bottom of the cart. She pulled out several towels.

"My bathroom has plenty of towels, thank you," Penelope said, hoping her impatience wasn't showing.

Mandy shrugged and shoved them back underneath the curtain of the cart. She continued on into the bridal bedroom. Pen followed her in, making sure to grab her purse as she did.

"What is it that Gary had to leave the card game for?" she asked, trying to sound as though she was nothing more than mildly curious.

"I don't know that it's my place to say, ma'am." Mandy cast a pert look her way before heading to the bed.

"Would this help?" Penelope had a five-dollar bill ready.

Mandy eyed it and smirked. "I don't think it would be fair to Gary for me to say anything."

This was more difficult than she thought. "You do realize he's been accused of killing Jiro Ishida, don't you?"

"I do," Mandy said, all hints of coyness replaced by a

surprising amount of animosity. She grabbed the first two pillows to set on the settee, her mouth pinched tight.

Perhaps Stanley was right when he'd insinuated there had been a relationship between her and Jiro. Did she think Gary had killed him?

The other maids had made it seem like she only went after big fish. Penelope supposed that, had Mr. Ishida been paid properly for his services, he'd have quite a nice amount with which to spoil a girl like Mandy.

"Okay, let's stop playing coy, and you can stop with the pillows. I'll give you twenty dollars if you tell me everything you know about why Gary left the card game, why he might have been meeting Jiro Ishida, and what your relationship with either or both of them is."

Mandy's head snapped up and she met Penelope with an incredulous gaze. "Relationship? Just what do you mean by that?"

"You tell me? Were you involved with either Gary or Jiro?"

She coughed out a sharp laugh, then her gaze narrowed. "A Japanese man? How dare you? Just because I'm a simple maid doesn't mean I would offer *those kinds* of services to someone like that. As for Gary, I think I can do a *little* bit better than a waiter."

"You seem to have misunderstood my questions," Penelope said in an apologetic tone, mentally kicking herself. "I didn't mean to insinuate anything of a sordid nature. There are different kinds of relationships, like perhaps those that are strictly business?"

Mandy's face went red and her eyes were wide. Penelope assumed it was due to embarrassment at being found out, until her nostrils flared with indignation.

"You snobby, rich women are all the same, if a maid isn't

stealing your jewels she must be doing something wicked with some man she has no business getting involved with... or really anyone that will take her, right?"

Penelope realized she had made a mistake trying to be so frank in this transaction. She figured Mandy was being coy as a way to get more money from her as Stanley had. Instead, she had obviously struck a sensitive spot. Even the suggestion of a business-like relationship seemed to upset the young woman.

"Again, I didn't mean to insinuate anything untoward between you and either Jiro or Gary. Forget I said anything about that. But can you at least tell me why Gary had to leave? What did you whisper to him?"

"If Gary got himself into trouble, it was his own fault," Mandy spat, going back to the pillows. She grabbed as many as she could and practically threw them on the settee.

Penelope exhaled with frustration, realizing this plan had completely gone astray. She should have factored in Mandy's pride.

She watched with muted frustration as the maid continued her duties of turning down the bedspread and drawing the curtains closed. When Mandy was done, she stood up straight, chin lifted and eyelids lowered with contempt. She walked toward Penelope.

"Will there be anything else, ma'am?" She said with barely constrained contempt.

"No, thank you," Penelope said. The twenty was already in her hand and it seemed vulgar to put it away now. Penelope figured the insult to Mandy was worth it and held it out to her. "For your troubles."

Mandy looked down at it and sneered with contempt. "Keep your money. I won't be needing it."

A sly, subtle smile came to her lips, even as her eyes

continued to glare at Penelope before she grabbed her cart and left.

Penelope stared after her in surprise. She heard the door to the suite open and close. Perhaps she had been far more insulting than she intended. Very few people would have turned down twenty dollars, even those who weren't "simple maids."

So what did she mean when she said she wouldn't be needing such a sizable amount? Was she coming into more money soon? Perhaps it had something to do with either Jiro's death or Gary's arrest.

At any rate, it would be impossible to get an answer out of Mandy now. That vault was securely closed. In fact, this pursuit had done nothing more than create more questions.

Penelope walked to the front door of the suite to turn the lock now that Mandy was gone. She peeked through the peephole to see if Mandy still seemed bitter about the interaction. Her brow rose in surprise when she saw Mandy in front of the door to the Honeymoon Suite. Was Bentley back in his room already? The question was answered when the man himself opened the door, puffing on another of his cigarettes and holding a glass of something that certainly wasn't water.

Pen couldn't hear what Mandy said to him, but a sly smile and assessing look came to his face. After a moment, he opened the door wider for her. She rolled her cart in, making sure her hips swung seductively from side to side as she did.

"Well, well, well," Penelope hummed with a smirk.

No wonder Mandy's uniform was so provocative. Perhaps she had altered it herself or deliberately chosen a smaller size. At any rate, she was certainly using it to her advantage. This might just be where she was coming into far more money than twenty dollars. Bentley certainly had a type, young and curvy.

"Poor Darlene," Penelope said as she headed back to her bedroom.

Pen walked into the bathroom to get a bath going. The large tub was perfect for soaking one's troubles away. She started the water, pouring some of the complementary scented oils in. A nice long bath before bed would be the perfect opportunity to organize her thoughts.

The scent of lavender, her favorite, filled the air. It also made her think about poor Gary, now probably in an uncomfortable jail cell that wouldn't smell nearly as nice.

As Penelope finished undressing and sank into the water, she pushed aside her guilt by telling herself that this would most definitely help clear her head so she could determine what really happened tonight.

After all, there were quite a few suspects to pick from.

CHAPTER EIGHT

THE NEXT MORNING, PENELOPE WOKE UP EARLY. SHE was momentarily caught in that same strange yet luxurious feeling she had when she had first spent the night in the apartment she had inherited from Agnes Sterling. For the three years prior to that, her sleep had taken place on a much firmer, lumpier mattress that she had almost become accustomed to.

Thinking about that reminded her to check in on Cousin Cordelia. She was the older first cousin of Penelope's father and the woman who had taken her in when he had cut Pen off financially.

Cousin Cordelia was meant to be her plus-one last night but had suffered some stomach ailment that had left her bed-ridden. In retrospect, it was probably a good thing since Penelope never would have gone down to play cards if Cousin Cordelia had been her guest.

Then who would be here to help Gary and discover who really killed Jiro?

After her discussion with Stanley and even Mandy last night, Pen had a feeling there was much more to this story.

In fact, she wouldn't have been surprised to find out Gary had been deliberately framed. Mandy seemed to have some hostility toward him, and Stanley made it seem like his connections involved their own dangerously tangled web.

But right now, she had more pressing matters. She checked the clock on the nightstand next to her bed and saw that it was seven in the morning. Not a horrid time to request something of Chives, the butler Penelope had also inherited from Agnes.

Penelope and Cousin Cordelia were still without a maid after the last one had been unscrupulously stolen from them—though not without a generous benefit in her favor, thanks to Penelope—so Chives had been the one to fill every need lately. Hopefully Cousin Cordelia, notoriously needy, hadn't been too much of a handful.

Last night, with nothing to wear, Pen had slept without a stitch of clothing on. It was no wonder she felt so energized this morning, she thought to herself with a grin.

Still, she couldn't very well wear the dress she'd worn last night. After last night's oil-infused bath, she abhorred the idea of putting on clothing that was badly in need of a good cleaning. Two hours in that cigarette-smoke-filled, crowded staff room playing a heated game of cards had left her dress rather sullied, as beautiful as it was.

Penelope's eyes fell to the silk kimono she had put on after her bath last night. She walked over and pulled it from the chair it was draped over. After slinking into it and wrapping it firmly around her waist, she went over to open the curtains. The hotel faced west, so the rising sun from behind the hotel was just beginning to brighten Central Park.

There was a phone in the living area of her suite. She went out and picked up the earpiece. Penelope first ordered

MURDER IN THE GARDENS

breakfast, something hearty with lots of bacon and eggs and toast. After that, she got the operator, and gave the number for her apartment.

While she waited for the connection, she pondered where to begin her day after breakfast. It was probably too early for Detective Prescott to have returned to the hotel, depending on what they had discovered last night. Perhaps the police had already cleared the rooftop to be opened once again? Pen doubted it, but it was at least worth a little bit of exploration to find out.

She heard the operator making the connection and before Chives could answer Pen spoke first.

"Chives, I hope I didn't cause any concern last night when I didn't return home. I decided to get a room at the Grand Opal Hotel. How is Cousin Cordelia?"

"Not to worry, Miss Banks, Mrs. Davies retired early and had a very recuperative night."

Penelope wasn't sure how to interpret that. Chives was always so overly tactful about things.

"She didn't keep you up all night with her demands did she?"

"No, Miss Banks. She was fine after several, ah, doses of her medicine."

Penelope grinned. Cousin Cordelia's "medicine" was nothing more than bootleg brandy. Her legitimate prescription had expired years ago, and they both simply ignored that fact when another bottle always magically appeared to replace an empty one.

"Well, tell her I'll probably be staying here at least another night. As such, I'll need a few changes of clothes." She rattled off the necessities. To his credit, Chives handled it with utter professionalism, even when it came to certain intimates. Pen didn't see the need for a full staff despite the size of the apartment. Still, it would be nice when her cousin finally settled on a maid, who should have really been the one to handle such a duty.

"Very good, Miss Banks. Shall I have them delivered to you?"

"I'm going to call Jane and see if she'd be interested in joining me here." Jane Pugley was Penelope's associate in her private investigation business. Pen had a feeling she would be thrilled about not only joining her on another big case but also getting a glimpse of the hotel. "There was a murder here last night."

"How terrible," Chives replied in his usual placid tone.

"Indeed. At any rate, if she agrees to come, I'll just have her pick the items up and bring them with her. If not, I'll call back and have you deliver them. It should be nothing more than a simple valise, I assume, and the hotel is only a few short blocks south of you."

"Very good, Miss Banks. And I will be sure to inform Mrs. Davies of your plans so she doesn't worry."

"Thank you, Chives."

Penelope hung up and noted the time. It was too early to call Jane without waking her on a Sunday. Idling around the suite seemed a dull business, especially considering everything that was going on in the rest of the hotel.

Had the police found more evidence? Witnesses? Clues?

There was a knock on the door announcing her room service breakfast. She ignored her state of dress and padded over to open the door. To his credit, the waiter didn't bat an eye at the fact that she was only in a robe. He dutifully set her meal, coffee, and orange juice down on the table by the window in the large open room. Pen tipped him before he left.

While she ate, she looked out at all the trees of Central Park. It forced Penelope's mind back to last night in the gardens, and filled her head with even more questions.

What had Jiro been doing up there after the party was over? Was he there to meet Gary? If so, why up on the roof?

Penelope knew she'd have to go up there and have a look. She stared down at the robe she was wearing, realizing that despite how much it covered—more than even her dress from last night did—it was highly inappropriate.

But who would even be up this early? After all, the only occupants of the hotel currently were those in the suites of the top levels.

That was enough to comfort her and she padded over to slip into her heels from last night. On her way out the door, she grabbed her room key. She opened it just enough to make sure no one else was in the hallway, then slipped out, locking the door behind her.

On the far side of the hallway, she could just barely make out a door that no doubt led to the stairwell. Opposite it was the staff elevator she had taken to the staff area last night.

As quietly as possible, she walked over and opened the door for the stairwell, and peeked in. Noting that, as expected, she had the stairs to herself, she slipped inside, just as quietly closing the door behind her. This was far better than waiting for either elevator, which might have someone inside.

Penelope craned her neck and saw that the stairs went up two more flights all the way to the roof. She rapidly ascended the first flight and paused on the seventeenth floor. After a moment's hesitation, she opened the door to that floor just a crack. That hallway was empty, so she snuck out.

There were only two doors on this floor, one to the Emperor Suite closest to the stairwell. This was supposedly where Genevieve was staying. The Presidential Suite was at the other end of the hallway, just above her suite. Penelope wondered who was staying there, if anyone. It certainly was convenient to the stairwell, only one floor below the rooftop gardens.

Something to keep in mind.

Penelope quickly but quietly escaped back into the stairwell. She went up the final flight and cautiously tried the door, which opened easily. It led her directly into the garden area with the bonsai trees. At least from here, she couldn't see the officious presence of any policemen so she boldly stepped out onto the dark, polished stone pathway. The lanterns that had been hung last night were gone, but it didn't matter. By now, the sun had risen enough that the entire garden was perfectly visible. While the magical ambiance of the night was gone, it was just as lovely in the daytime. However, Penelope was only focused on one area of the gardens.

She quickly approached the centerpiece of the gardens, the koi pond. Detective Prescott had said something about Jiro being drowned. Being the only water feature, this must have been where he had died.

It looked so harmless, only a few feet deep. The fish continued to swim, oblivious to the horror that had taken place overnight. Whatever joy the beautiful scene gave her, it was quickly eroded by the mental image of Jiro lying there dead.

Why had Gary been holding his body? Surely he would have run if he had been the one to kill Mr. Ishida. That lent credence to the idea that he had been trying to help him rather than murder him.

All the more reason to find the true killer.

"Hey! What do you think you're doing here?"

Those shouted words snapped Pen out of her thoughts. Her eyes flashed to the police officer coming from the tea house.

"No one is allowed up here—" He stopped when he saw what she was wearing, his eyes widening as they traversed the length of the robe. "*Ma'am?*"

"I'm sorry, I must have taken a wrong turn in the stairwell!" She exclaimed in an easy manner, offering an apologetic smile. She spun around and headed back toward the door from which she came.

"Wait just one moment!" he called after her.

Penelope was inclined to simply continue on, but something caught her eye—or rather the lack of something did. She stopped and stared at the bonsai garden. It was long enough for the policeman guarding the roof to catch up with her.

"Now see here, ma'am, you can't just—"

"There's a tree missing," she interrupted, pointing to one of the pedestals. The pedestal was bare, missing the tree with pink flowers.

The one that had looked like a tree made just for a doll.

CHAPTER NINE

"I'm afraid I can't let you leave the premises, ma'am. Not until one of the detectives comes up and clears you."

The policeman had at least allowed Penelope the dignity of taking her inside the teahouse while they waited for one of the detectives to appear. She was sincerely hoping it would be Detective Prescott rather than the other. Pen subconsciously adjusted the kimono more firmly around her body.

"I honestly don't see what bother it would be for me simply to go down to my room and change."

"Perhaps you should have thought of that before trespassing on a crime scene dressed like...*that*." His eyes flitted down to her robe then quickly darted away, filled with embarrassment.

Really, it was quite preposterous!

"Shouldn't you have been guarding that door all along? Why was there no police officer to stop me?"

"The New York Police Department has better things to

do than waste men playing nanny to a garden," he scoffed, rather defensively.

"And the missing tree? It could be related to the murder! I know for a fact it's quite delicate and valuable."

"Oh yeah, and just how would you know so much about that tree, ma'am?" He asked giving her a suspicious look.

Penelope realized she had stuck her foot in it, and wisely decided not to say anything further.

Pineapples!

The door was opened and Penelope was pleased to see Detective Prescott's face appear, handsome as ever. Though, this morning it sported quite the perturbed expression.

His eyes blinked for a moment, as though making sure he was seeing what he was.

"You're wearing...a robe."

"Good eye," Penelope teased, looking overtly impressed. "You should be a detective."

He breathed out an impatient sigh.

"Oh, don't be too scandalized, it's pretty enough to wear in public." She spun in a circle to show it off. "It's a kimono. Isn't it the berries? I'm thinking of stealing it. Just in case you felt like arresting me for a crime I'm actually guilty of."

He cast a hard look toward the policeman. "You kept her up here dressed like this?"

A surge of pleasure ran through her at how ardently he came to her defense. He really was very handsome when he was angry. She almost felt a bit bad for the policeman who began swallowing and stared back at him like a stunned deer.

She might as well diffuse the situation.

"Not to worry detective, it's terribly comfortable, even

with absolutely nothing on underneath," she said, offering a daring smile.

Penelope positively reveled in how uncomfortable they suddenly looked. It served the policeman right, treating a woman in such a manner. As for Detective Prescott, she was rewarded with the slight tightening of the jaw that told her he wasn't quite immune to her charms.

She walked over to a chair at one of the tables and sat down. The kimono slipping open to reveal slightly too much unstockinged leg was inadvertent but she didn't do anything to remedy it.

"That's hardly decent!" the policeman protested.

"Applesauce, women show far more at the beach these days. Don't give me such a scolding look."

Detective Prescott gave her a more cynical expression. "Perhaps he's thinking of the uproar that might ensue when I have to take you away in handcuffs."

She sat up straighter and snatched the silk cloth right back over her legs with indignation. "What on earth for?"

"How about interfering with a police investigation?"

"I was doing no such thing. As I told this police officer, I simply took a wrong turn."

"Odd, I can understand one not knowing their left from their right, but most people are adept at distinguishing their up from their down."

"I suppose that makes me special," she said with a smile, hoping that would earn her some favor.

It did not.

Detective Prescott sighed and removed his hat to run his hand across his dark hair, a sure sign he was irritated.

"Perhaps rather than waste time scolding me, you should be investigating the missing bonsai tree? It may have something to do with Mr. Ishida's murder. Perhaps a motive?"

"We discovered the missing tree last night. We still haven't been able to locate it. All it does is point the finger at your...friend."

"Really? How?"

"Some of the soil left in the base was found on his clothes."

"And was there any soil on Mr. Ishida?"

The look on his face told him that indeed there was.

"I thought so, which means it could have easily been transferred when Gary tried to rescue him."

"Or tried to drown him."

"Is that all you have?"

"The scratches on his arm that look like claw marks. It shows signs of having been in a struggle."

"Oh, I can explain that one. I was with him when he sustained those cuts. We were in the pagoda just next door.

Detective Prescott's brow furrowed.

"He was retrieving something and a gardening tool scratched him. It resembled claw marks. In fact, there are several witnesses who can attest to the fact that they were there before he even went up to the roof. Again, is that all?"

"He had quite a large amount of money on him. He's invoked his right to remain silent so none of this has been explained."

"Again, I can explain for him. As I told you last night, we were playing poker and he had just won quite a large pot."

"It seems you have an answer for everything."

"And it seems your evidence against him is dwindling. All the more reason to start looking at other suspects?"

MURDER IN THE GARDENS

"There's still a button we found in the pond, ripped from his shirt."

"I see, well...that could have come off when he pulled Jiro out of the pond, perhaps to see if he could still be saved?"

"You seem awfully unwilling to believe it might be Mr. Garret. Sometimes the most likely suspect is often the guilty party."

"Well, you seem awfully willing to point the finger at him without considering the idea it may not be him."

"I'm not, surely you know me better than that. I fully plan on questioning everyone you mentioned last night and looking at all the evidence objectively. Or at least I should be instead of battling with you."

"I'm not battling, I'm offering alternate theories so you and your flat-footed colleagues don't dig your heels in to focus only on Gary," she said testily.

The officer got ruffled feathers over that one, standing up more erect and glaring at her. Even Detective Prescott seemed angry.

"That's not fair, Miss Banks."

She backed down. "You're right, I apologize for that. I just want to make sure justice is actually served. So often those with the fewest resources are easily scapegoated. But I must confess that with you on the case I feel more reassured."

"Since I know there is no point in asking, or *demanding* that you not get involved, if you happen to discover something that takes the blame off Mr. Garret, I'm more than happy to consider it. Likewise, if I find something that does the same, I'll be the first to champion his release. Until then, he remains in custody as our prime suspect."

"I do know that Jiro Ishida hadn't yet gotten paid for his

work here. In fact, it was quite a source of contention between him and the owner of the hotel, Genevieve Walton, which anyone observing them last night could see."

Detective Prescott studied her. "How do you know this?"

"You'd be surprised what you can pick up from the staff."

"Especially when you question them after being told not to interfere."

"I simply had a conversation with the bellhop who escorted me to my room last night, nothing more. Have you questioned Mandy, the maid who was the one who got him to leave to go to the roof?"

"Yes, we have."

"And? What did she have to say."

He simply stared back at her, his eyes filled with incredulous amusement.

She glared back. "Fine, moving on. You should know that the stolen tree was quite popular last night."

"How so?"

"The couple in the suite on my floor, Mr. Green and his date, Darlene? She was positively smitten with it. She wanted him to buy it for her. I was told it was an azalea species, almost two hundred years old and quite valuable."

The police officer snorted with disbelief. "How much can a tiny tree be worth?"

"Hundreds according to what I've heard."

He coughed out an incredulous laugh. "What a load of—"

"Thank you, Officer Brooks," Detective Prescott said, then turned back to Pen. "How is it you know so much about this tree, Miss Banks?"

"A man who seemed to be an expert on the matter last

night at the party told me. No, I don't have a name, he wasn't particularly engaging."

"Well, we're obviously looking into why this tree was stolen and its possible relation to the case. Anything more?"

"Perhaps Mr. Ishida caught someone in the act of trying to steal it? Maybe there was a struggle and they pushed him into the koi pond where he hit his head? That could explain how dirt from the plant got on him and then Gary. Or, as much as I hate to say it, perhaps Mr. Ishida himself was stealing it and got caught by someone trying to stop him. Though, I certainly wouldn't blame him, if indeed he wasn't getting paid for his services."

"That's a lot of supposition."

"But certainly worth investigating."

Detective Prescott studied her, then heaved a heavy sigh. "I suppose I should at least get you back down to your room so you can change into something...decent. Then you'll be coming with me to give a formal statement."

"I have nothing else to wear."

"What were you wearing last night?" he asked pointedly.

"In bed?" Penelope responded, batting her eyelashes. The officer cleared his throat and smirked. Detective Prescott wasn't so easily amused.

"I mean the dress you were wearing."

"Detective," Penelope began in a scolding voice. "You can't honestly expect me to go down to the lobby wearing the same dress I was in last night. And escorted by you? Whatever would people think?"

Detective Prescott gave her a wry look.

"We can just as easily have this interrogation in my hotel room. Unless you intend to get physical." She offered him a provocative grin.

The police officer now stared at her as though she were a wanton harlot, which she found amusing.

"Miss Banks, need I remind you that this is a murder investigation."

"And I'm trying to help you investigate."

"Very well." He turned to the officer next to him. "Thank you, Officer Brooks, I can take it from here."

The look he gave the detective indicated exactly where his mind went at that suggestion.

"Let's take the stairs," Penelope suggested. "The elevators are intolerably slow."

Penelope led Detective Prescott down two flights and then opened the door that led out to the hall where her suite was located. She continued on until she got to her door.

"You're in the *Bridal* Suite?"

Penelope turned to bat her eyelashes at him and smile. "Don't worry, it was simply a matter of convenience. Don't go getting any ideas."

"It wasn't that, I just—never mind." His jaw hardened with annoyance, which made Penelope smile to herself as she opened the door.

Before entering, she turned around and in a lowered voice said, "At the end of the hall you have the Honeymoon Suite. That's where Bentley Green and his, ahem, *girlfriend* for the evening, Darlene, are staying. I'm not sure who's in the Oriental Suite." She gestured toward the door in the middle of the hall.

With that, she opened the door and led Detective Prescott inside.

He took a moment to admire the interior, then turned to her. "You mentioned Darlene had an interest in the azalea tree?"

"Yes, she was quite taken with it last night. That could

have just been the simple infatuation of a mind that's too easily impressed. Or, who knows, it could have been something more? You should also find out the name of that fellow I mentioned, the one who told me the value of the tree. He seemed to be a bit of an expert on the Far East."

"But you don't have a name?"

"No, but I do remember exactly what he looked like."

"Of course you do," he said, his mouth ticked up into a smile. "Was there anything else that you remember, or that you learned during your overnight stay?"

"Only that if Genevieve did in fact pour all her money into this hotel, it was very much worth it, don't you think?" Penelope glanced around, then turned to gauge his reaction.

Detective Prescott cast a quick glance around the sitting area and nodded. "It is indeed very nice," he said in a blunt tone.

Heaven forbid he be a romantic, Penelope thought to herself, not without some amusement.

"Oh, there is one more thing! Mandy just happened to be the one who turned down my bed last night."

"Was she?" Detective Prescott asked in a cynical voice.

"Pure coincidence," Penelope said in an airy way. "However I figured since she was here I might as well ask her more about what happened last night."

"Did you?" he asked just as cynically.

"I did, but you'll be happy to know she wasn't at all forthcoming. In fact, I couldn't even bribe her to tell me anything."

"*Miss Banks*," Detective Prescott sighed with exasperation.

"What? It certainly works better than whatever interrogation tactics you police officers use. But as I said she wasn't forthcoming. *However*, she did mention that she wouldn't be needing the money."

"What does that mean?"

Penelope gave him an exasperated look.

He nodded with understanding. "She'd soon to be coming into quite a bit of money of her own."

"Even twenty dollars couldn't tempt her," Penelope said

The amount had his brow raised. "Really?"

"Really. I also know that after my room, she went right to the Honeymoon Suite."

"Perhaps she was there to turn down their bed as well."

"Or something more devious? Now, do you want to tell me what she whispered in Gary's ear last night?" she chanced asking.

Detective Prescott studied her. "I'd rather not encourage you by answering that question."

"How would that be encouraging me?"

He gave her a sardonic look.

"Okay," she conceded. "But perhaps I can help put it into context for you? Furthermore, your answer may convince me that Gary is in fact guilty and I should just drop this entire endeavor." She suggested with a coy smile, wondering if he remembered the significance of that particular word.

The subtle smile that came to his lips and the slight glimmer in his eyes told her it did.

Penelope absently brushed back her hair as she always did when her flirtatious mood was overshadowed by something more powerful.

"I seriously doubt telling you will either convince you that Mr. Garret is guilty or keep you from becoming involved with this case."

MURDER IN THE GARDENS

"Don't be like that. I always thought we worked well together."

Before he could respond, there was a knock on the door, which surprised them both.

"Are you expecting anyone?"

Penelope shook her head. "Not at all."

"Well, let's find out who it is," Detective Prescott said, not without some suspicion and caution.

CHAPTER TEN

Detective Prescott deliberately went ahead of Penelope to open the door. She was amused to realize he was blocking the way for her own protection. She wasn't sure if it was out of concern for her safety, or for her state of dress—or rather, lack thereof.

"Why, Detective Prescott, whatever are you doing here?" she heard a familiar voice say on the other side.

Penelope peeked her head around past his shoulder and saw Cousin Cordelia standing there next to a bellhop carrying two pieces of luggage. So it seemed her cousin planned on spending the night.

"I could ask the same of you, Cousin Cordelia," Penelope said, pushing her way past the detective. "I see you're feeling better this morning."

Cousin Cordelia was too dumbstruck to answer. Her eyes wandered down Penelope's body, taking note of the fact that all she had on was the kimono. Then her gaze shifted to detective Prescott, now filled with umbrage.

"I see that I've *interrupted* something," she accused.

Penelope laughed. "Don't be silly, Cousin. Detective Prescott was just, *ahem*, interrogating me."

She should have been ashamed of the suggestive way she said that but it was too enjoyable watching everyone's reactions, including that of the bellhop.

"Really, Penelope," Cousin Cordelia exclaimed, pushing her way into the suite. "I see it's a good thing that I insisted on bringing your things with me personally or at least having Leonard bring them here with me. I just know you've gotten yourself into trouble somehow. Imagine walking around your own hotel room dressed like that when there is a killer about!"

As though Pen wasn't safe in her own room, even with a detective.

"As for you, Detective Prescott, I must say I'm rather *unimpressed* with the lack of professionalism from your police officers. They treated me like a perfect *criminal* when I tried to enter the hotel, blocking my way at every turn, as though I was here to commit some crime. Fortunately, a Mr. Dickens, the hotel manager himself, came to my rescue. Of course, with him, I had to be rather *insistent* about what I had come for. I apologize Penelope for betraying your confidence. Once I explained to him that you had, er, nothing to wear he was more than agreeable about allowing me to come up."

"Of course," Penelope said.

Cousin Cordelia paused, stopping at the end of the foyer once she saw the rest of the suite. "Oh my, it really is lovely isn't it?"

Now Penelope understood. Cousin Cordelia was never one to be left out of anything. Last night she had been devastated when she was too sick to join Penelope at the party and get a first glimpse at the gardens. No doubt, when she had learned Chives was gathering clothing to be sent to the Grand Opal Hotel for Pen, she decided to come along herself, if only to see what she had missed. All the better if there was a tawdry murder added to the mix, information she had obviously pried from him.

The bellhop cleared his throat and then entered after her. "Where would you like me to put these ma'am?" He looked first towards Cousin Cordelia and then to Penelope.

"The one on the left goes in the bridal bedroom," Penelope said sweetly. "The other in the other bedroom."

That wrestled Cousin Cordelia's attention back towards the couple still standing by the door. She studied them with narrowed eyes. "I realize these are *modern* times and what is going on here is really none of my business. Just inform me that my presence isn't wanted and I'll be more than happy to leave."

"Nonsense, Cousin," Penelope said gliding in to wrap an arm around her cousin's shoulder. "When is your presence ever unwanted? As I said, Detective Prescott was simply here asking me a few questions about the, ah, incident that took place last night."

"And yet you still chose to stay here, all while I had taken to my sick bed near death! If you're looking for a murderer, detective, that Elizabeth Dower should be arrested. I knew she was ill at the last auxiliary meeting despite her protests. It's a wonder I'm not in a coffin as we speak."

"But look at you now, in the pink of health. All the better to enjoy this fabulous hotel suite. Isn't it just divine?"

That cheered her cousin up a bit. "It is rather lovely. How was the party last night? Was the garden everything they said it was? Would it be too early to have a look now?"

Penelope's eyes drifted to Detective Prescott. "I'm afraid the gardens are unavailable at the moment."

"Whatever for? Surely one can simply go up and look?"

"That's where the body of Mr. Ishida was found."

Cousin Cordelia's hand came to her chest in horror at the mention of murder again. Penelope gently guided her to the sofa where she could take a seat. She wondered if her cousin had thought to pack her "medicine."

"Oh, Penelope, why do you always embroil yourself in such morbid affairs?"

"I certainly hadn't planned on murder, Cousin."

Detective Prescott cleared his throat cautiously walking towards them. "I was just about to take my leave, but I would like you to join me in the lobby at your earliest convenience, Miss Banks. Once you are dressed appropriately of course. This man you were talking about from last night? Perhaps you can describe him to the manager of the hotel. He might know who the individual is and give me a name."

"Of course, detective," Penelope quipped, standing back up. "But first, I need to wire the payment for this room."

Penelope picked up the phone to connect with Mr. Wilcox via the operator. She instructed him to remit payment to the Grand Opal Hotel. While she had the phone, she also called up Jane who, as expected was delighted at the prospect of joining her, even if it was for work on a Sunday.

After her calls, Pen headed to the bedroom to get her purse to tip the bellhop. She came back out to find Detective Prescott getting upbraided yet again by Cousin Cordelia for allowing such sordid things as murder to happen in a fine hotel for decent people such as herself.

Pen didn't pity Detective Prescott having to remain with her agitated cousin while she went back to her room to get dressed. To his credit, he seemed to be taking it with good grace; there was even a slightly amused tilt to his mouth.

Once Penelope was dressed and had applied just the right amount of makeup, she came back out to find Cousin Cordelia sagged against the couch, now in a near faint, eyes closed. Apparently, she had exhausted her complaints.

"There is tea service for you, Cousin," Penelope said pointing to the bar. "Perhaps you can take it with your *medicine*?"

One of Cousin Cordelia's eyelids shot open in alarm. She pursed her lips with displeasure that Penelope would suggest such a thing in front of the detective. Penelope grinned and turned her attention to Detective Prescott.

"Shall we?"

There was a mild look of relief on the detective's face as he readily agreed with a nod. He was the first to leave the room. Penelope followed, taking her key with her. While they waited for the elevator Penelope turned to him with an amused look. "You aren't worried about your reputation after that encounter, are you?"

"I trust that your cousin didn't get the wrong idea about us."

Penelope laughed. "Of course she did, but that's Cousin Cordelia for you. She lives for gossip, particularly the sordid kind. But not to worry, I'll correct any *untoward* assumptions she might have about us."

"Why thank you, Miss Banks," Detective Prescott said in a dry voice.

The elevator doors opened, and they were greeted by Darlene staring out at them in mild surprise. A hesitant smile came to her face. She lifted the box in her hands that had "Gregory's" printed on it, and her smile brightened.

"Just a few donuts for Mr. Sleepyhead," she said as she exited.

Penelope and Detective Prescott made way for her. She could see the fob attached to Darlene's key dangling from one hand pressed against the side of the box. It was done in the same intricate design as hers, complete with a tassel, only hers was in red instead of white.

As soon as the doors closed, she and Detective Prescott made eye contact.

"That was Darlene. She was up and about awfully early," Penelope mused.

"Perhaps she was just getting donuts."

"You're awfully credulous. Who's to say she wasn't selling an azalea plant on the black market?"

"Or she was just getting donuts."

Penelope made a disgruntled noise.

Detective Prescott chuckled.

"I *do* plan on questioning her and Mr. Green, if that pleases you."

"Well, that's a relief, otherwise I would have had to do it myself."

Now, it was Detective Prescott's turn to make a disgruntled noise.

"Yes, yes, no interfering with your investigation," she sang in a low voice.

Once in the lobby, Penelope noted that there were still several policemen lingering about. Her eyes wandered and she saw through an open archway that the Lotus Blossom restaurant already had patrons sitting down to breakfast.

The lobby itself was empty, but outside there were still members of the press, just as there were last night. That certainly couldn't be good for business.

At the front desk, Wendell Dickens looked as though he

had been particularly taxed already this morning. Her Cousin Cordelia must have been even more difficult than usual. Penelope *almost* felt sorry for him.

Mr. Dickens saw them approach and his expression briefly deepened with irritation before he seamlessly smoothed it out and greeted them with a smile, no doubt realizing that one member of the couple was currently staying in the Bridal Suite.

"How can I be of service this morning Miss Banks? Detective?"

Before the detective could speak Penelope interjected. "I see that the restaurant is open for breakfast?"

"Yes, Miss Banks, it opens at seven every morning."

"Does the restaurant serve donuts?"

Mr. Dickens looked at her as though she had asked if the restaurant hired dancing monkeys as waiters. Once again, he quickly ironed out the look of incredulity and offered a tepid but indulgent smile. "We are more than happy to accommodate our hotel guests' needs and wants, particularly those inhabiting one of our suites."

"So if I had called and asked for donuts you would have been happy to purchase some and have them sent up?" she confirmed.

"Yes," he managed to eke out. Not exactly "happy" about it, but still willing. "In fact, there is an establishment only a block away, Gregory's. Would you like me to send out for some?"

"Oh, no thank you, I was just curious." She gave Detective Prescott a meaningful look.

"Now that we've established that," Detective Prescott said giving her a harsh look back. He turned back to Mr. Dickens. "I was wondering if you could help us determine the name of a man who was a guest at the party last night. He's a person of interest in this case."

At the mention of the case, Mr. Dickens's eyes widened with panic, then darted around only to realize there were no guests nearby. He relaxed somewhat, then gestured for them to follow him to a more secluded spot.

They were tucked into a corner of the lobby far away from where anyone might accidentally run into them, or worse, hear the conversation. Detective Prescott turned to Penelope and indicated that she should begin describing the man.

"He was at the party last night, an odd-looking fellow. He seemed to be an expert on the bonsai trees and had a particular fondness for eastern culture. He was a few inches taller than me, slight build, exceptionally dark hair, and blue eyes. He was dressed rather well, I imagine he has money."

"What made him seem odd?" Detective Prescott pressed.

"His eyebrows."

"His eyebrows?"

"Yes, they were...straight."

"Straight?"

"That's the only way I can describe it. It gave him a rather severe look, making them seem almost...exotic perhaps?"

"Ah, I think I know the gentleman you are describing," Mr. Dickens interjected. "That would be Mr. Hubert Combs. He was an advisor of sorts in the development of this hotel, specifically with regard to Oriental authenticity. He's an expert on the Far East."

"Do you happen to have an address on file for Mr. Combs?"

MURDER IN THE GARDENS

"Yes, of course, but I should point out he happens to be residing on the same floor as Miss Banks, in the Oriental Suite. Though I can't imagine he had anything to do with Jiro's death."

Penelope and Detective Prescott looked at each other, then back to Mr. Dickens.

"So he was here last night after the party?"

"I presume so."

"He also didn't seem very happy that you had included bonsai trees in the garden," Penelope said.

"Yes, Mr. Combs has rather...elevated opinions about these things."

"He was a snob," Penelope confirmed.

Mr. Dickens tactfully cleared his throat rather than answer.

"Was there anything special about the missing azalea plant? Something that he would know about?" Detective Prescott asked.

A look of horror came across Mr. Dickens's face. "The azalea tree is *missing*? That was one of our more valuable inclusions. Miss Walton is going to be positively devastated. It took quite a lot of care to get it here all the way from Japan. The flowers are quite delicate you see. Are you sure it's...*gone*?"

"Yes. You didn't notice it missing when you found Mr. Garett and Mr. Ishida?"

He gave Detective Prescott a distracted look. "I was too stunned by what I saw, Gary holding Jiro's body. My most immediate concern was contacting the police, obviously."

Before any of them could speak again, Detective Prescott heard someone call his name. They all turned to see the other detective from last night rushing over to meet him.

"You'll never believe what happened," he said with a disgruntled look on his face. "Our suspect? He's been released. Some muckety-muck out there obviously wants this case swept under..." He glanced at Penelope and then pulled Detective Prescott further away so they were out of hearing distance.

Penelope tempered her annoyance. No matter, she'd somehow finagle the information from Detective Prescott eventually. She and Mr. Dickens watched, waiting until the animated detective had finished explaining everything to Detective Prescott. Finally, he pulled off his hat and ran his fingers through his hair. Then, he walked back over, looking perfectly confounded.

"Does this mean Gary is going free?" Penelope asked.

Detective Prescott sighed. "It seems they're ruling the death an accidental drowning."

"*Really?*" she exclaimed.

"So it would seem there is no need for the police presence any longer?" Mr. Dickens queried, looking tactlessly relieved.

Detective Prescott gave him an irritated look, then sighed again. "It would seem so."

"Wonderful, it will be nice to have my hotel back again. I can't imagine what all this fuss has done to our image, and just when it's opened!" He gave the detective and Penelope a sour look.

"There is still the matter of the missing azalea that we should look into."

Mr. Dickens narrowed his eyes. "I believe our insurance company will be able to handle that matter, thank you. As the manager of this hotel, I feel very confident in informing you that we are no longer in need of the services of the New York Police Department."

He gave Detective Prescott one last warning look before excusing himself back to the front desk with a satisfied expression on his face.

Penelope kept her attention on Detective Prescott, studying him. "You don't think it was accidental, do you?"

He met her with a level gaze. "I most certainly don't."

"Well, then, it would seem you may need my help after all, detective."

CHAPTER ELEVEN

"I assume this means you're no longer *officially* investigating the case?" Penelope asked Detective Prescott.

"As far as New York City is concerned there no longer is a case," he said, looking angry. "I suppose you'll be happy now that Gary is free."

"Nonsense, as I stated, I believe in justice. Mr. Ishida deserves that just as much as Gary did."

He gave her an admiring look.

"Though, I suppose I wouldn't be *meddling* if I were to keep investigating at this point," Penelope confirmed.

"We *are* still talking about a murder, Miss Banks."

"Shouldn't you call me Penelope now that this is no longer an official case, *Richard*?" Penelope asked, her smile growing.

Despite the circumstances, Detective Prescott still managed a smile. "You really do like trouble, don't you?"

"I really do like *justice*," she said pointedly.

His smile faded. "So do I."

"Then come up to my suite. We can sort this out up

there and decide what to do next, because I certainly don't plan on leaving it at this."

She could tell he hated the idea of involving her, but at this point, he was out of options, and she did still have a suite at the hotel.

"If only to keep you from getting yourself into more trouble."

They had to pass by the front desk in order to get to the elevators. When Wendell saw Detective Prescott was joining Penelope upstairs he quickly scurried over to stop them.

"I thought I made it clear that your services were no longer required, detective. I'm afraid the hotel rooms are for guests only."

Penelope took hold of Detective Prescott's arm. "Richard is my guest."

Wendell gave Penelope a disgruntled look. "It's my understanding that you *already* have a guest in your room, one for whom you have yet to pay. I had the pleasure of meeting Mrs. Davies this morning." His expression took on a bitter twist, as though unfavorably remembering the encounter, before he continued. "There is an additional fee for extra guests. And if you have any more coming, the hotel will need their full name for record-keeping purposes. I should also point out that the, ah, *Bridal* Suite has only *two* bedrooms," he hinted.

If he was hoping to embarrass her by not so subtly insinuating something, he had no idea who he was dealing with.

"I'll be more than happy to have my lawyer wire whatever additional fee is required for *all* guests. But surely you wouldn't deny a bride the company of her fiancé in her own bridal suite, would you?"

MURDER IN THE GARDENS

She felt Detective Prescott go tense. The muscles of the arm to which she clung flexed in a rather pleasant way.

Mr. Dickens gave her a look that was dripping with skepticism. "So the detective that just so happened to be handling Jiro's death is also your fiancé?"

"Quite fortuitous, isn't it?" Penelope said with a dazzling smile and a wink. "Now if you don't mind, Richard and I have a lot of, ah, making up to do."

Richard exhaled something incomprehensible.

Wendell looked positively vexed, but he realized there was nothing he could say or do. Penelope continued on before he could find some way to prevent them. She held onto Richard's arm the entire way, not letting go until they were inside the elevator car. Once there he did the work of freeing himself from her grasp.

"Am I that odious?" she asked in a teasing voice.

"No, but you definitely are that troublesome. Was it really necessary to pretend you are my bride-to-be?"

"It seemed rather fitting considering the suite I have." She studied him as a thought suddenly came to her. "You aren't otherwise *engaged* are you?"

Something flashed in his eyes, and Penelope suddenly had the horrid realization that he might in fact be engaged, in the most problematic sense of the word.

"No, I'm not otherwise engaged," he said, his jaw hardening. It made his scar ripple. She had the sense that she'd said something to make him angry. Rather than pursue it, she left it alone. While this bit of acting was no longer fun, it certainly had become more intriguing. Detective Prescott knew all about her failed romance with Clifford Stokes. Penelope knew absolutely nothing about his past relationships.

She decided to change the topic.

"Why do you still think it was murder?"

Richard visibly relaxed and looked thoughtful. "I saw Mr. Ishida's body last night before he was taken away. There were signs of a struggle, and only the upper portion of his body was wet. If he was alert enough to struggle then he was certainly able enough to pull himself out. Which meant, someone was holding him in the water." Something sparked in his eyes and he suddenly reached out to press the button to take them to the rooftop. "There's something I want to investigate."

Penelope felt her excitement begin to build. He was willingly incorporating her into a case for once.

Having already pressed the button for the sixteenth floor, the elevator stopped on that level and the doors opened for them. Straight ahead was the Oriental Suite. They remained in the elevator, but both of them studied it noting that Hubert Combs was still a guest in that suite. As the doors closed, Penelope felt that Richard certainly agreed he should be their next stop after the visit to the gardens.

"Perhaps now you can tell me what it is that Mandy said to Gary to get him to the roof."

Detective Prescott thought on it for a moment then turned down his mouth in acknowledgment. "I suppose I could. She said that a member of the band, a man named Sam Trebant wanted to meet with him to discuss something. She didn't know what it was. We've been trying to get in touch with this Mr. Trebant but we haven't found him yet."

Sam? Penelope knew he had been upset about losing at poker but did he lure Gary up to the roof in order to frame him? Had Sam killed Jiro? If so, why?

Then again, perhaps Mandy had simply made it up, using someone she knew was familiar to Gary?

MURDER IN THE GARDENS

When the doors opened again on the rooftop level, the officer was near the pond, flicking water to disturb the koi.

"You do realize a man was murdered there just last night?" Detective said by way of introduction.

The officer nearly fell over into the pond in startled surprise. Penelope coughed out a laugh. It served him right. He corrected himself at the last minute and spun around, an initial look of anger on his face. It vanished when he realized he saw Detective Prescott.

"Is there a new development, sir? Something you need me to do?"

Detective Prescott sighed in resignation. "It seems you're relieved of duty, Officer Brooks. This is no longer a crime scene."

The officer looked surprised, then pleased. He shrugged his shoulders and sauntered past them to the elevator, casting one quick glare at Penelope as he went.

"What are we looking for?" Penelope asked once the officer was gone.

Detective Prescott squinted out at the gardens. "Any evidence of what may have happened. That's why I came back this morning, to review the scene in the light of day.

He slowly walked toward the pond. Now that it was fully daylight, the gardens seemed so serene and pleasant, almost defying the violence that had taken place the night before.

"He had a sizable head wound on the back of his head. Those usually bleed pretty heavily," Detective Prescott said, his eyes scanning the scenery. "I can't see him accidentally hitting the back of his head and then falling into the pond in a way that he could have drowned, not with only half his body wet. I'd like to at least know on which of these rocks or hard surfaces he may have hit his head. There should be some evidence of blood somewhere. Last night even with flashlights it was too dark to tell."

They both started in the most obvious place, the rocky waterfall above the koi pond. From there they worked their way further out.

"Ah-ha!" Penelope heard Detective Prescott announce behind her. She spun around and hurried over to where he stood near the garden with the stream made of pebbles. He was staring at the large, rough boulders rising from the side portion. It was about as tall as Penelope, and she leaned in to take a closer look. There was definitely blood on the craggy surface.

"That isn't very much, is it?"

"No, it isn't. There should be a lot more than this." His eyes fell to the ground, following the trail of blood that would have led to the pond; a trail of blood that wasn't there.

"It's quite a ways away from where he drowned," Penelope noted. "Could he have hit his head and then wandered over in a daze and fell in?"

"That seems *highly* unlikely. Even if he did, as I said, there were signs of a struggle. His fingernails indicated he at least clawed at something to try and get out. Besides, who cleaned up the blood after the fact?"

"So, someone either bashed his head against this rock or pushed him and he fell into it. Then they dragged him all the way over to the pond to drown him?"

"So again, where is the blood?"

Their eyes fell to the ground.

"The walkway is slate with some kind of sealing on it, probably to avoid permanent stains."

"Like blood," Penelope said.

"I doubt the owners had that in mind. But it worked for

our murderer's purpose."

"So someone came back to clean it, maybe to make it look like an accident on Jiro Ishida's part?"

"Perhaps someone with access to cleaning equipment, like a member of the staff?" Detective Prescott said pointedly.

Penelope knew what he was hinting at. Gary certainly had that kind of access. "That still opens the door to a lot of people. Any member of the staff, really."

"Including Mr. Garret."

"Golly, Richard, if I didn't know any better, I'd say you were jealous. At least now I know what kind of husband you'd make."

"I'm remaining objective. I'm perfectly willing to consider that he didn't do it. I firmly believe in innocent until proven guilty. Which is why I focus on the evidence. Most notably the fact that *he* was indeed found with Mr. Ishida's body in his hands."

"What about motive? Why would Gary kill him?"

"As I said, he was smart enough to keep his mouth shut. He knows his rights."

"And because of that, he's guilty?"

He sighed. "No, of course not. In fact, the little evidence we had hardly makes a case."

"See?"

"In fact, this insistence on claiming the death as accidental makes me think there's much more at play here. Someone powerful has inserted themselves into this, and I doubt they'd do it for the sake of a waiter."

"Well, in the spirit of honesty, I should point out that he does tend to be a young man who knows a lot of people. He struck me as one who likes to curry favor. Could he have pulled in one of those favors?"

Detective Prescott considered that, then shook his head. "Also in the spirit of honesty, I don't see how. We took him straight to the station and he made no contact with anyone. How would they have known? I got the feeling it was more about wanting this murder to go away than anyone looking out for his welfare."

"So someone involved with this hotel then?"

"Someone with serious connections."

"Well, that's probably a few people."

"I suppose it's time to go have a talk with Mr. Combs." Detective Prescott headed toward the elevator and Penelope followed.

"Wait just a moment," she said, looking down at the Zen garden as they passed. "The sand has been disturbed."

"Yes, I noticed it last night but didn't get a very good look at it, being that it was dark and all. I assumed it had happened sometime during the party, as it was so far from the pond. Mr. Dickens couldn't confirm if it was like that before he returned to the roof and found Mr. Garret with Mr. Ishida's body."

"So it could be related," Penelope said, walking over. "It's kind of an odd disturbance, don't you think? Like someone deliberately wiped their hand through it."

"Looking at it now in the daylight, it does appear that way. So, perhaps they either did it out of spite or to cover their tracks. Say, because they had on distinctive footwear? Or...maybe they were searching for something."

He reached into his coat and pulled out a pen. He used it to comb the sand, carefully pushing it aside and scanning the result.

It didn't take long before both their eyes landed on something gold.

CHAPTER TWELVE

Detective Prescott plucked the tiny gold item out of the sand, and held it up so they could both inspect it.

"That certainly looks familiar," Penelope said.

"Does it?"

Penelope nodded. "It does. Let's go back downstairs. We have someone to interrogate, it would seem."

Detective Prescott carefully pocketed the gold item and followed Penelope to the elevators.

When they got to the lobby, Penelope led him to the front desk. Fortunately, Wendell Dickens wasn't lingering anywhere nearby, even better, he didn't seem to be in the lobby at all. She approached the young man sitting behind the desk and offered her most charming smile.

"I was wondering if you could help me. I found a key in the hotel and I have no idea to whom it belongs." She pulled out her own key with the white decorative rope and the tassel to show him. "It looks like this except it's gold, complete with a gold tassel? Do you know what room that key would open?"

His brow rose in recognition. "Oh yes, it would belong

to either our Presidential or Emperor Suite. Those are the only rooms with gold attachments on the keys. Do you have the key with you? I can hold onto it for our guest."

"You know I plumb forgot it. It's still up in my own suite, but I'd be more than happy to take it up one little flight to give it to the person in the, ah, Presidential Suite?"

Pen knew that Genevieve Walton was inhabiting the Emperor Suite. She was hoping this young man would tell her the other occupants of that floor.

"Oh, that's no problem, ma'am. It's probably better that I take it. I don't think Mr. Dickens would like it if we had the guests doing our work for us." He laughed good-naturedly.

Penelope just sighed internally. "So, as far as you know they haven't checked out yet? After all this unfortunate business, I would have understood if they did."

"As far as I know they haven't. In fact, no one has, which is surprising."

This was getting her nowhere. Detective Prescott seemed to realize this and he leaned in to intervene.

"I'm one of the detectives who worked on the case from last night. I need you to tell me who is in any room that might have a key with a gold tassel."

That had the young man's brow rising even higher. "I, um, well I suppose I could tell you that much. Miss Genevieve Walton is in Emperor Suite and Robert Paxton, the golfer, and his wife, they're in the Presidential Suite." He leaned in conspiratorially. "They're staying at no cost, courtesy of Miss Walton."

"Thank you very much, young man," Detective Prescott said. He flashed a subtle, taunting smirk Penelope's way as they turned to head back to the elevators.

"That was cheating, you know."

"I didn't say anything that wasn't true. I *was* working

on the case. He doesn't have to know there's no longer a case. Not everything has to be extracted using your womanly wiles. Sometimes being direct is the easier route."

"You make me sound as bad as Mata Hari herself. Perhaps next time I'll come to the front desk wearing nothing more than a beaded brassiere and transparent silk skirts, maybe even showing my navel."

Detective Prescott flashed his eyes towards her, widened slightly. They inadvertently wandered down her body and then back up to her face where they were met with a teasing smile from her.

"Detective Prescott, are you undressing me with your eyes?"

He blew out his mouth and a grimace came to his face. "This isn't productive."

Penelope laughed softly. "Oh, I don't know, I find it quite enlightening."

They passed by the Lotus Blossom restaurant and someone caught Penelope's eyes. She stopped Detective Prescott, taking hold of his arm and turning him to face the entrance of the restaurant.

Inside sat Betty Paxton, idly staring out the window in deep thought.

He took a step to go ahead of her but Penelope stopped him.

"I think this one is better handled with my womanly wiles. Trust me."

Detective Prescott considered her for a moment, then silently nodded. Still, he arched an eyebrow as though to say that she shouldn't hesitate to seek him out if her method didn't work.

She nodded with understanding, then continued into

the restaurant. Betty didn't acknowledge her approach until she was right at the table for two.

"It's such a terrible business isn't it?" Penelope said offering a distraught expression as she boldly took the second chair without waiting to be invited to sit. "I can't believe Jiro Ishida is dead."

She noted the key resting on the table, complete with the gold rope design and tassel attached. She couldn't tell if a part of the tassel was missing.

Betty's eyes fluttered with surprise and irritation. "I'm sorry I—"

Penelope continued before Betty could ask her to leave. "You're Betty Paxton, no? The famous golfer's wife? I heard him mention last night that you had hoped to have Jiro create a Japanese garden for you down in Georgia."

Betty's hand came up to her chest and she fiddled with the neckline of her dress. She swallowed hard, and a sad look came to her eyes before she dropped them to the table.

"Yes, I had hoped..." she left off the rest of the sentence rather than finishing it, as though she couldn't.

"Had you ever met with Mr. Ishida before last night's party?"

Her eyes snapped back up to Penelope in a mild panic. "What do you mean by that?"

Penelope pursed her lips and paused, as though wondering whether or not she should proceed. "It's just that I saw you and Mr. Ishida talking to each other at the party last night. Quite familiarly."

Now the panic in Betty's eyes seemed to triple. "I don't know what you're trying to insinuate. I was simply complimenting the man on his work, that's all. Jiro was..." Her voice faltered a bit as she continued. "He was a master at what he did. He deserved better than this. Better than the way they..." She seemed to come to her senses and her mouth snapped shut before she finished.

Penelope tried not to seem too eager as she waited to see if Betty would change her mind and continue. Who were "they?" And what did she mean by better than this? Did it have to do with him not getting paid? Or was it related to the murder?

Penelope decided to try another route in getting an answer. "I ran into your husband last night in the lobby. The police wouldn't let us go back to our rooms. He must have been gone when the murder happened. I suspect to a *speakeasy*," she leaned in to whisper the last bit. "He was rather ossified."

The animosity came flashing to Betty's eyes. It was the most animated Pen had ever seen the woman get, other than how she had been with Mr. Ishida last night.

"What my husband gets up to at night is none of your affair. And I would appreciate it if you would leave me be."

"I was simply wondering why he and Bentley Green were arguing, is all." Penelope studied her to see if that sparked anything by way of either knowing or surprise.

Betty's nose wrinkled with distaste, as though she was familiar with the man's reputation, but her expression also indicated she had no idea that there'd been any reason for a disagreement between the two men.

"Did they know each other before? Or perhaps they met this week while staying at the hotel? I see that you're in the Presidential Suite, one floor above Bentley Green's suite." Penelope's eyes fell to the key on the table.

Betty's gaze hardened as she stared at Penelope. "What exactly is it you're after, Miss...?"

"Banks, Penelope Banks. And I was just wondering if you heard any commotion on the roof last night. Anything that might indicate when the murder actually took place? If so, what time was that?"

Suddenly, the panic was back in her eyes. Rather than answer, she shot up from her seat, grabbing her key as she did. "I...I—have to..."

"Or perhaps you were there on the roof yourself," Penelope quickly said before she could flee.

Betty inhaled sharply and her face went perfectly white. Penelope thought for sure she was going to faint. Instead, she stuttered a few more incomprehensible words, then she fled.

Only to be met with Detective Prescott.

Penelope sighed and slowly got up to follow and meet with them at the entrance. It seemed he had a point about being more direct. It was obvious Betty had something to hide.

It was time to figure out what that was. Directly.

"Mrs. Paxton," Detective Prescott said quietly but firmly. "I'm one of the detectives handling Mr. Ishida's murder. I do need you to answer a few questions for me."

This was uttered gently enough that it had a calming effect on Betty, though she still looked as white as a ghost. Her eyes darted back and forth between Penelope and Detective Prescott, then she seemed to sag and numbly nodded.

Detective Prescott led her to a secluded set of chairs in the lobby and sat her down across from him. Penelope took the third chair, pulling it closer so they didn't have to raise their voices.

Behind Betty, Pen saw Mandy getting off the main elevator, despite being in a uniform. She was holding what looked like a garment bag, covering the front part of it.

MURDER IN THE GARDENS

Mandy furtively cast her eyes around the lobby before stepping off and quickly rushing over to the stairway.

Pen dismissed it, turning her attention back to Betty.

Detective Prescott pulled the single thread from a gold tassel out of his pocket and showed it to Betty Paxton. "Do you recognize this?"

Betty's eyes fell to the key in her hand and she blinked rapidly.

"I...." She paused long enough that Detective Prescott had to urge her to continue.

"Just tell me what happened Mrs. Paxton. Mr. Dickens already informed me that it was you who alerted him to go to the roof. But perhaps it wasn't quite as you stated? If Mr. Ishida's death was an accident, you could likely avoid prison."

Betty's eyes flashed back up to him in alarm. "I didn't kill him! He was already dead when I got to the gardens."

Both Detective Prescott and Penelope were taken aback by that confession.

Richard was the first to recover. He leaned back in and met Betty with a steady gaze.

"Mrs. Paxton, tell me everything that you know."

She held his gaze and swallowed as though regaining her composure before she continued. "I went to the roof—just to take another look at the gardens of course," she said quickly. "I had been very impressed with them, and I wanted to enjoy it without all those people around. So I went up and...that's when I saw him, lying there in the fountain."

Her hand came up to her chest again and she looked more green now than white. The expression on her face was one of genuine horror and grief. But that didn't mean she

COLETTE CLARK

hadn't caused his death. Guilt could potentially elicit the same response.

"How did this thread from your key end up in the sand of the Zen garden?" Detective Prescott said holding up the gold thread.

Betty eyed the thread as though it was her personal foe. Her eyes slid back to Detective Prescott. "I heard someone else on the roof while I was up there. I panicked, thinking it was the killer. That must have been when I stumbled back into the sand. Before you ask, no I didn't see who it was. They were on the other side of the roof. But I did hear the door to the stairwell open and close. That must have been how the killer got away. It's why I took the elevator down the one flight instead of just taking the stairs."

"The sand looked as though someone tried to wipe away any evidence of being there."

"My key fell when I stumbled. I dug around trying to look for it. I noticed my prints from my heels there as well, so I smoothed those out. But that wasn't to cover up any evidence, at least not out of guilt from having *killed* Jiro. I just didn't want anyone to know I'd been up there. After finding my key, I tried to smooth it over is all."

"You didn't want your husband to know you were up there," Penelope said, studying her.

Betty's eyes snapped to Penelope with indignation. "I do wish you would stop insinuating things like that. Jiro and I were not having an affair or anything of the sort. I respected his work and him as a...gentleman," she said in a lofty manner.

Penelope felt the first trickle of doubt. She had thought for sure there was something more intimate going on between Jiro and Betty, but now she wasn't so sure, at least when it came to an affair. "Still, your husband doesn't seem like the type that would like even the insinuation of an affair. You and Mr. Ishida alone on the roof at the same time?"

"I already told you I went up there to see the gardens, that's all. I certainly hadn't expected to run into him...like that." She swallowed hard again. "As for my husband, he was gone by then. The only reason he *deigns* to come to New York is because he enjoys the speakeasies. Otherwise, he'd never set foot north of the Mason-Dixon Line."

How convenient, Penelope thought.

"So it's purely coincidence that Mr. Ishida happened to be up there at the same time you decided to get another view of the gardens?"

"Yes," she snapped at Pen.

Detective Prescott shot Penelope a look and she begrudgingly sat back, allowing him to take over once again. He turned his attention back to Mrs. Paxton.

"How long did you wait in between finding Mr. Ishida's body and calling down to Mr. Dickens?"

She paused for a moment. "Perhaps twenty minutes or so. I wasn't even sure about calling at all. I knew that would involve me in this, but I just thought of poor Jiro up there on the roof like that. I couldn't bear thinking about it."

"What I don't understand is, why you made up a story about hearing something on the roof rather than just admit that you found his body?"

Betty cooled her gaze. "For the exact reason I'm sitting here with you two. I knew how it would look. Unwarranted insinuations," she said, casting a villainous look towards Penelope, "or worse, accusations of possibly being the murderer myself."

"Why did you choose this hotel to stay at?"

"We were gifted the hotel room," she said, matter-offactly as though she had nothing to hide on that count. "They told us that the offer was for publicity's sake. The truth is, usually for an appearance at an event such as last night's party, Bobby would get paid. He is very popular," she said in a slightly resigned voice, as though his popularity was one of the things Betty least liked about her husband. "He has a tournament in Long Island on Thursday. I was the one who insisted we stay here in exchange for nothing more than a room because I wanted to see the gardens. I'd seen the botanical gardens when they were first done last year, and I was curious to see how Jiro would reinvent it for a rooftop hotel." She cast a cool look Penelope's way. "I *briefly* met him then, the last time we were here. Any supposed *relationship* we had was nothing more than that of an artist and admirer."

She said it with deliberation, but Pen could see the emotion in her eyes. They were filled with a sadness that bordered on despair. Penelope flitted her gaze to Detective Prescott and could see him studying her with the same lingering suspicion.

"If you're looking for someone who may have had any motive for murdering Jiro, then you should look at the owner of this hotel or perhaps the manager, I don't know. I *do* know that they refused to pay him for his service, and after all that *beautiful* work he did. Honestly, the way he's been treated here, it's an insult. We don't deserve him. Now he's..." She stopped, looking as though she might cry.

She quickly recomposed herself and met them with a steely look. "As for my husband, I trust that you will leave him alone. I won't have you questioning him in this manner. As I stated, he has a golf tournament on Thursday, and he needs his rest and recovery."

Especially after last night, Penelope thought.

"He had nothing to do with Jiro's death." Betty shot Penelope a hard look. "And he certainly has nothing to do with *Bentley Green*," she added, practically spitting his name.

Betty stood up. "If I'm not under arrest, I'm leaving. If you have any further questions for me or Bobby you can go through our attorney."

With that, she left.

"Well, that was productive," Detective Prescott said in a dry voice.

Penelope smiled at him. "Actually, it was quite productive."

He arched an eyebrow questioningly.

"Two things," she began. "One, she obviously knows who Bentley Green is, more notably his sordid reputation. Which means she might know why her husband may have been arguing with him. Two, she only referred to Jiro Ishida by his first name, not *Mr. Ishida*. Rather familiar don't you think, especially for nothing more than a so-called admirer?"

"Do you still think they were having an affair? I didn't sense that from her."

"No," Penelope said thoughtfully, "but they were definitely much closer than she wanted us to know. I'm just wondering why she was so reluctant to admit as much."

"It's going to be difficult to talk to her or her husband now," Detective Prescott said. "That leaves us with two options, Hubert Combs or Bentley Green."

CHAPTER THIRTEEN

Detective Prescott and Penelope rose from the seating area to head toward the elevators. Before they could get there, Jane strolled in through the front doors, her eyes wide as she admired the lobby of the Grand Opal Hotel.

"Jane!" Penelope called out. "You're here, thank goodness. You can join us upstairs."

Pen looked around, happy to see that Mr. Dickens still hadn't made an appearance in the lobby. By now, she had three additional people joining her in the suite and she didn't want to have to deal with his pesky interference just as she was about to continue with the case.

"Oh, Miss Banks," Jane sighed as Penelope looped her arm through hers and guided her toward the elevator. "Isn't it lovely?"

"Yes, it is. A shame that such nasty business has taken place."

"Oh yes, the...*murder*," Jane said, whispering the last word. Her eyes brightened as they alit on Detective Prescott following them. "Detective, you're here too? Is this one of your cases?"

"It seems there is no longer a case. They've determined the death was an accidental drowning," he said in a disgruntled tone.

"Oh," Jane said her brow wrinkled in confusion, no doubt wondering why she was here.

"Of course Richard and I are under no illusion that it *wasn't* a murder that took place," Penelope clarified.

Jane's eyes darted back and forth between the two of them, probably noting how familiar Penelope had been with the detective's name. Detective Prescott grimaced slightly but said nothing.

They arrived on the sixteenth floor and headed toward the suite.

"The Bridal Suite?" Jane asked in surprise. She gave them an amused smile. "Isn't it bad luck to see the bride before the wedding?"

"There is no wedding, Miss Pugley. In fact, this whole idea of us pretending to be a couple seems foolhardy," Detective Prescott said in a resigned tone.

Penelope laughed. "The good detective seems to consider such subterfuge rather *untoward*," she said as she unlocked and opened the door.

They found Cousin Cordelia sitting on the couch with the entire tea service spread out before her. She stared down at the magnificent array of offerings like a child in a toy store, wondering which one to choose.

"Cousin, look who's come to join us. It's Jane, you remember my associate. She can keep you company, perhaps help you decide which tea to choose? The detective and I have some business to conduct in the meantime."

"Hello Jane dear," Cousin Cordelia said distractedly. "Penelope, if you go back downstairs perhaps you can ask that they remove some of these orchids, at least from my bedroom and bathroom. I'm all for floral scents but this one isn't to my liking at all."

Pen sighed, used to how picky her cousin was. Soon she would be protesting the quality of the sheets or the lighting through the windows.

"It may be a while, we're still conducting interviews."

"I'll go down," Jane offered.

"Bless you Jane dear, at least someone here is looking out for my welfare."

Penelope rolled her eyes and grinned at the equally amused Detective Prescott as they exited and closed the door behind them.

"I think it would be better to start with Hubert Combs," Penelope said. "We could possibly eliminate him as a suspect unless there's something he's hiding that gives us reason to think he might be involved. I have a feeling Bentley is far more entangled in whatever is going on in this hotel, what with his interactions with Jiro, Mandy, *and* Bobby Paxton, not to mention whatever business he was concerned with at the party."

"You may have a point. We'll start with him."

Penelope smiled and went directly to the Oriental Suite. She was the one to knock on Hubert's door. After a moment he opened it just a peek, looking out at them with a questioning and imperious gaze.

"How can I help you?"

Penelope decided to do Detective Prescott the favor of not having to pretend he was acting in an official capacity. She knew how finicky he was about his ethics.

"Hello, I'm Penelope Banks. I don't know if you recognize me from last night? I'm with Detective Prescott here, investigating the unfortunate death of Jiro Ishida. I wanted to ask you about something you said last night, About the azalea tree?"

"Yes?" He asked in a nasal voice.

"The tree has been stolen, and—"

"It has? Have any of the other trees been stolen?" he demanded, interrupting her.

Penelope realized she had hooked him. Rather than answer his question, she used it as a segue to get them into his suite.

"Perhaps it's best if we discuss this inside?"

She could see the conflict on his face as he debated whether or not it was worth letting them in. Finally, he sighed and then opened the door wider.

Penelope blinked as he came into view. He was wearing a silk robe almost similar to the kimono she had been wearing this morning, long with large armholes. However, his was all black and was tied with a wide belt around his waist. It didn't look like the one the hotel offered. Penelope figured it was his own personal robe.

She looked beyond him into the suite that was revealed as he led them further inside. This one was fully facing Central Park. It had a darker theme than her suite, mostly black and gold. There was a mural on one wall of koi fish done in gold, swimming among black lilypads. The furniture was more masculine but still very eastern with shiny black surfaces and carved dragons.

Mr. Combs had his own tea service out but his teapot was flat and round, made of dark clay, also not anything like that in her room, which was all white.

He sat down on his sofa and Penelope and Detective Prescott politely took the chairs across from him. He didn't bother offering them any tea. Instead, he picked up his cup with both hands. It was round and small, matching the color of the pot, and had no finger hole by which to hold it.

"So, again, have any of the other trees been stolen or gone missing?"

"No, just the azalea tree."

He relaxed and sipped his tea, seemingly no longer interested in what she had to say.

"Last night you remarked that the tree was rather valuable and old? Could that be why someone may have stolen it?"

He turned down his mouth as though she had said something absurd. "I don't know why. It's hardly the most impressive specimen in the garden. In fact, the condition it was in is rather insulting to the art of bonsai."

"How so? It seemed fine to me."

He gave her a withering look. "Of course it seemed fine to *you*. However, I'm an expert in these things, Miss Banks. I could tell that the tree hadn't been well cared for. Probably a product of irresponsible transportation from Japan, and incompetent care during its tenure at this hotel. Frankly, it makes me wonder if any of the others are even worth it."

Penelope wasn't quite sure what that meant but she wanted to stay focused on the azalea plant. "Can you think of *any* reason why anyone would want to steal it?"

"None at all. I, myself, would have chosen any other specimen—were I so inclined."

That's just what someone who wanted to take the suspicion off themselves might say, Penelope thought to herself. She eyed Detective Prescott and could see that the same thought was running through his head.

Hubert Combs wasn't a fool, though. He studied both of

them, his mouth twisted into something resembling amusement. "Ah, I see how it is now. You think I was the one to take it, lying about how poorly it was cared for. If so, where exactly would I be hiding it?"

"You tell us? Did you take it?" Penelope questioned.

"No."

"What *exactly* was wrong with it that made it such a poor choice for stealing?"

He sighed and set his cup down, as though they had just requested an oral dissertation. "A number of things. It wasn't getting the nutrients it needed, the flower petals were already wilted, the leaves were faded instead of vibrant green, there was far too much soil, and frankly, it had a lingering odor to it, no doubt from rot."

Penelope hadn't been close enough to the tree to smell anything, but she did remember Darlene recoiling slightly after leaning in towards it. Then again, perhaps that was the smell she hadn't been able to place last night.

"Could the smell have been an effect of the flowers dying? Many flowers give off a particular scent when they become wilted and dead."

"The flowers of that particular Japanese azalea tree don't have a scent. That was the first indication something was wrong. Any serious bonsai enthusiast would have known right away and turned their nose up at it. The fact that the thief chose that one instead of the juniper right across from it is beyond understanding. That one is far older and far more valuable."

She looked at Detective Prescott to see if he had any other questions.

He was staring at Mr. Combs thoughtfully. "You said something about wondering if the others were even worth it."

There was a glint of amusement in Mr. Combs's eyes as he narrowed them Detective Prescott's way. Penelope now understood what it was about his face that made him seem so odd. Although it was quite obvious he was a white man, he had somehow manipulated his eyebrows so that he would seem to have eastern features resembling those of a Japanese man. She wondered if he dyed his hair a darker shade of black as well. The man certainly had an obsession with the Far East, or maybe just the Japanese.

"You've guessed me out, detective," Mr. Combs said in an almost prissy manner. "I was offered my pick of the entire collection of bonsai trees just this morning."

"The *entire* collection?" Penelope said with a gasp. "By whom?"

"By the owner, Miss Walton, of course."

"Why is she selling?"

"Why does anyone sell?" he said giving her a sardonic look.

"Is the hotel in trouble?"

"*That* is beyond my knowledge." He lifted his cup and took another sip of his tea.

"Are you going to buy any of them?" Detective Prescott asked.

Hubert pursed his lips and thought. "Considering the condition of the azalea, I'll have to do a more thorough inspection, but my initial observation leads me to believe that the others are in fine condition. I *do* plan on being discriminating, of course. I only have so much room in my Newport home. Still, it's quite the curated collection. This hotel has turned out to be quite the prize. Miss Walton is as much an admirer of the Japanese as myself though, so I suppose that's to be expected."

Of course she would have to be in order to put so much

Japanese detail into this hotel. Penelope had to admit the result was exceptional. But she was more focused on eliminating Mr. Combs as a suspect.

"What is it you admire about the Japanese?" she asked pretending to have nothing more than idle curiosity.

The way his eyes steeled, the blue blazing with fire, told her almost everything. He gave her another withering look.

"You Americans and, frankly, most people in the western world seem to underestimate other cultures to your detriment. Granted, most of them are still quite primitive and not worth indulging, but I've been to Japan, Miss Banks. In fact, I've been to many parts of Asia quite often. Japan is the one to keep an eye on. I've spent quite a lot of time there among the Japanese people. I admire their traditions and way of life. There is a certain pride and ceremony in the way they do almost everything. In many ways, it's a shame that they have decided to modernize as much as they have, though it is understandable. Even up until the later part of the last century, their army consisted of Samurai."

Upon seeing her confused expression, he gave her a patronizing look. "The warrior class, somewhat like the knights of the medieval age, only not nearly as boorish. There was an...elegance to how they fought.

"Even with modernization, I suspect their traditions will hold. They will be a formidable force on the world stage, and be forewarned, they are just as imperialistic as the western world is. This new law our *esteemed* Congress, in all its wisdom, decided to impose against them will do us no favors."

"New law?" Penelope asked.

"I assume Mr. Combs is referring to the Immigration Act that went into effect last year."

"Or what you might call the Asian Exclusion Act," Mr. Combs concurred, with narrowed eyes. "The law effectively bars any immigration from Asia. There was a decidedly anti-Japanese tinge to the whole affair. I can tell you that Japan was *not* happy about it."

Once again Penelope reminded herself that she needed to learn more about politics. After her last major case, she realized how important local government was and made sure to read the papers about what was going on in the mayoral election this year. It seemed national and international politics should be included as well.

What was it so many people had against immigrants? She found the diversity in New York fascinating. All one had to do was look at the beautiful garden above them to see how much other cultures contributed to the city.

Still, she couldn't see how it related to this case. Jiro Ishida wasn't even an immigrant. Surely that law wouldn't affect natural-born citizens?

At any rate, she couldn't think of anything that made Mr. Combs look guilty. He seemed to have no animosity towards Jiro, and as far as the azalea tree, he hadn't even been interested in it. Further, it seemed he now had the opportunity to buy the entire collection of bonsai trees.

Which created an entirely new line of inquiry.

Why was Genevieve Walton suddenly so willing to sell a part of the garden that had only just been completed?

"Thank you for your time, Mr. Combs. You've been quite helpful."

"Anything to help, detective. Although I wasn't in favor of Mr. Ishida's attempt at modifying authentic Japanese culture to accommodate the lowly American palate, I was an admirer of his. His loss is a tragedy to the world."

Being that Detective Prescott had no further questions, Penelope was all too happy to escape the suite with him. Something about Hubert Combs' interest in Japan was a bit much.

"So, what do you think?" Penelope asked once they were back in the hallway.

"I think, he should probably just move to Japan, though I pity the Japanese if he does. There's a fine line between admiration and obsession. Still, I didn't get the sense that he was guilty of anything."

"Nor did I. So, shall we move on to Bentley Green?"

He nodded and they walked to the end of the hall and knocked on the door to the Honeymoon Suite. To both their surprise, it was opened by a maid. She wasn't one that Penelope recognized, but those from last night were probably home during the day.

"We'd like to talk to the occupants of this room," Penelope said.

"Oh," the maid said. "They've already checked out, a few hours ago in fact. That's why I'm here to clean it. I guess they got spooked by the death and all; they were supposed to stay all week."

Penelope and Detective Prescott eyed one another. Bentley and Darlene must have left right after Darlene brought up the donuts. Now, more than ever they needed to talk to them. They quickly went to the elevator and waited for what seemed like ages before it came. The two of them quickly got on to take it down.

When the doors opened to the lobby, they were taken aback by the sense of chaos that filled the air. Somewhere they could hear the sound of crying, and the staff were all huddled in groups whispering among themselves.

Wendall Dickens had reappeared and was the first to notice them.

"Detective!" He rushed over with urgency. "You must come quickly, there's been another body. Mandy Clarkson, one of our maids has been *murdered*."

CHAPTER FOURTEEN

Detective Prescott straightened up in surprise at the news that Mandy had been murdered. He quickly followed Wendell to a corner where a woman was hunched over, her body shaking with sobs.

Penelope followed behind them, even though it was now clear to her that this was going to be an "official" case once again. Detective Prescott would probably ask her to keep her distance.

As they approached she realized she recognized the maid from last night. It was Rosie, though she wasn't in uniform. Even though her face was in her hands as she cried Penelope could recognize her petite, curvy body and the dark bobbed hair.

"*Rosie*," Wendell practically snapped at her. Penelope frowned at his back. He wasn't being very considerate, especially if Rosie had been the one to find her fellow maid's body. "This is a detective. He's going to ask you about what you found, *particularly* what you were doing in the rooftop gardens. You know staff, even out of uniform, isn't allowed up there."

Penelope glared at his back. He really was a tyrant of a boss.

Rosie slowly pulled her head away from her hands and looked up at Detective Prescott with an expression of despair on her face. Penelope felt her heart seize in sympathy. She remembered the first time she'd seen a dead body. It wasn't a very pleasant experience, especially if one knew the person. Rosie sniffed and tried to collect herself, sitting up straighter as she focused her attention on Detective Prescott.

He sat down in one of the chairs next to her and leaned in, a gentle look of concern on his face.

"You were the one to find Mandy?" he asked in a soft voice.

Rosie nodded. "Yes, sir, only a moment ago."

"Up on the roof? In the gardens?" Detective Prescott confirmed.

She sniffed and shook her head.

"Actually, she was in the staff elevator. I was—" She gave Mr. Dickens a quick, sheepish look. "Coming down from the gardens. So, I called the staff elevator, And she was just...lying there with one of those letter openers from the rooms coming out of her chest."

Detective Prescott snapped his head to Mr. Dickens. "I assume you've called the police?"

"Yes, of course. But I just assumed since you were here—"

"And the elevator, you've stopped it? Made sure all the staff know not to use it?"

"Naturally. It's paused on the roof."

"Right," Detective Prescott interrupted, standing up. "I have to go and secure the scene, make sure no one disturbs it any further."

He turned his attention back to Rosie and his face softened. Penelope could still see the look of consternation in his expression. He no doubt wanted to bring Rosie with him if only to have complete control over all the parts of this new crime. But it was obvious that she would be a complete mess if she were taken back to the roof.

"I'll stay with her and make sure no one disturbs her," Penelope offered.

He wasn't quite happy about that either. Still, he sighed and nodded. Then turned back to Wendell. "You come with me."

"But, ah, would it be at all possible to escort Rosie to a more *private* area perhaps?"

Penelope once again resented his lack of tact, but she could understand his position. The hotel was getting a bad enough image as it was, with one death. Now there was a second. A crying maid in the lobby didn't exactly instill confidence in any future or current guests.

"Do you have an office of some sort on this floor?" Penelope asked.

His expression indicated that he found that idea abhorrent, but he then seemed to see reason. "Yes, I suppose. It's behind the front desk. You can take her there."

Penelope gently put her arm around Rosie's shoulders and urged her from the chair, then led her behind the front desk. She turned to the employee working the desk who was openly gawking at them as they passed. "Do you think you could have some tea sent in?"

He continued to stare for a second, then blinked and nodded, standing up straighter at attention. "Of course ma'am."

Penelope opened the door and went into the small office then closed it behind her. It was a small, sad windowless space. There was a chair at a desk and another one next to it. She wondered how many employees had received a dressing down in here. She led Rosie to the chair at the desk, which was more comfortable, then she took the other one.

"I know how upsetting this must be for you," she sympathized.

That brought a fresh round of tears from Rosie. "I just saw her last night, right after I had changed into my clothes after leaving that poker game. She was grabbing some stuff for her shift and said she was surprised to see me here so late."

"You had stayed past your shift?" Penelope asked just to get her talking about something other than the murder.

Rosie sniffed up her tears and gave Penelope a sheepish look. "Well, yes...mostly to watch Gary play." Her cheeks went red, and Penelope understood. After all, even Penelope had thought Gary was attractive, if perhaps a bit too boyish for her tastes. Rosie was young enough to be smitten.

"I just don't understand it, who would kill Mandy? I know she wasn't the most likable person but...*murdered*?"

"How was she not likable?"

"Well," Rosie suddenly wore a guilty expression. "She had a habit of...doing things, kind of underhanded things, to get her way, you know?"

"Such as...?"

Rosie heaved a sigh. "I really shouldn't speak ill of the dead."

"It may help us find out who killed her," Penelope offered.

Rosie's mouth twisted with conflict then she nodded. "Well, for example, she made sure she was scheduled to cover the floors on the upper-level suites when the hotel fully opens. That's where the wealthiest guests stay, and they leave the biggest tips. She flirted a lot, especially with Mr. Dickens. With him, all you have to do is wiggle a little and he's like soft butter."

That explained his preference when it came to maids, Penelope thought wryly.

"But Mandy also liked to find people's secrets and things, you know? She would listen at doors and things like that. I once caught her going through our cubbyholes downstairs, where we keep all our stuff during our shifts. That's why I never leave anything valuable in them, just my change of clothes. I hate that it's all out in the open like that. This morning I got here to find out someone had spilled hooch all over mine, *pumpkin pie* flavored from the smell of it!"

Penelope's brow wrinkled in bewilderment. Pumpkin pie? Having visited more than a few speakeasies in her time, she'd seen all manner of flavored cocktails. Frankly, pumpkin pie liquor sounded delicious.

"I guess I could understand it though. The booze flows like water down in the staff area. We might as well open our own speakeasy," Rosie giggled, then became somber again. "Still, you'd think they would have at least been considerate enough to give it a good rinse before I started today. I had to do it myself!"

"What were you doing on the roof?"

"Well, usually before my shift, I go up there and smoke a cigarette. We're not supposed to. Mr. Dickens don't like the staff to be up there, not unless we're actually working. And we can't smoke in the stairwell either. If we get caught, we're automatically fired. Most of us slip out the back door of the staff area to the alley behind the hotel. But the garbage is back there and it smells something awful." She wrinkled her nose in disgust.

"Anyways, I figure, since I'm still in my day clothes, being that I had to let my uniform dry, I can sneak and go to the roof. I took the main elevators since the staff elevator takes forever. Mr. Dickens doesn't allow us to use it, especially if we're in uniform."

So that's why Mandy had been so furtive earlier this morning.

"None of us even use the staff elevator lessen we're going up to the suites or the roof, on account of how long it takes. So I rinsed out my uniform and I took it up to the first floor, then switched to the main elevators to go to the roof, 'cause it's quicker. I was thinking the sun would help dry out my uniform and maybe the air would get some of the smell out. I'd be fired for sure if Mr. Dickens smelled gin on me.

"So, I got to the roof, no problem. Had my cigarette, and when my uniform was a little drier, I called up the staff elevator. It's the only one that goes all the way down to the basement. Then the doors opened and—"

She swallowed and went pale.

"That's when you found Mandy," Penelope finished for her. "Did you notice anything else? Anything about...Mandy's body?" Pen asked hesitantly.

Rosie's face crumpled as though she was going to cry again, then she sniffed and sat up straighter. "She wasn't in uniform. In fact, she was wearing a really pretty dress, looked kind of expensive. It was light purple with big blue flowers on it, kind of like those watercolor paintings."

A new dress, one that looked expensive? Perhaps Mandy had already come into her money and decided to go shopping. So what was she doing back at the Grand Opal

Hotel—particularly, what was she doing dead in the staff elevator? Maybe that's the dress she had been carrying in the garment bag earlier.

There was a knock on the door and Penelope stood from her seat to answer it. A young waiter was holding a tray with tea service.

"You can just put it on the desk." She led him over and cleared a space for it. As fastidious as Wendell was with running the hotel, his desk was just as rigidly neat but still cluttered. She pushed aside orderly stacks of forms and envelopes for him to set the tray down. Her eyes settled on one for a company called Burnside Development. That must have been one of the companies that helped construct this hotel.

Once he was gone, she placed tea bags in each of the cups and poured hot water into them. "How do you take yours?"

Rosie gave her an apologetic smile. "I actually don't really like tea very much." Penelope stared at her for a moment then grinned. "I suppose I should have asked, shouldn't I have? I don't like tea either."

That at least got a small laugh out of Rosie. Penelope laughed with her and sat back down in her chair.

There was another knock at the door, this time followed by the door opening before Penelope could even stand up. It was Detective Prescott. Apparently, the police had arrived now and he was ready to take over once again.

He cast one scrutinizing look Penelope's way, as though he knew she had been questioning his witness. He softened his expression as he turned to Rosie. "I'm going to need you to come with me, miss."

Rosie nodded and rose, flashing a quick smile Penelope's way as she followed Detective Prescott out.

"As for you Miss Banks, by now you know the rules."

Pen sat back in her chair and crossed her legs. "Yes, detective, I'll no longer be *meddling* in your case."

"But I do thank you for your help, all the same," he said with a smile.

When he left she frowned and sagged in her chair. It had been enjoyable working with him as a partner. Now that she was once again on her own she pondered what to do with herself. Bentley Green and Darlene were the two most obvious suspects, which meant Detective Prescott would be starting with them.

Penelope had other options.

Most notably, she figured a certain former suspect might soon be fully processed and released from jail at this very moment.

Perhaps she could give Gary Garret a ride home.

CHAPTER FIFTEEN

Penelope rushed back to her suite to use the phone to call for Leonard, her chauffeur. Jane and Cousin Cordelia were cheerily sipping their tea and chatting. She was loath to break up the happy pairing but, as Sherlock Holmes would say, the game was afoot!

"I hate to ruin the day with more bad news but it seems as though there's been another murder in the building. One of the maids."

Jane's eyes widened but, having worked for Penelope for a few months now, she wasn't too visibly unsettled at the news. By now, she would have been perfectly used to murders, as macabre as that idea was. To be fair, so should Cousin Cordelia, but the poor dear did have a nervous constitution.

"Oh me!" her cousin cried falling back on the sofa. "I knew it. I had a strange, ominous feeling as soon as I stepped foot in this hotel. Oh, if only I had thought to bring my medicine with me!"

Penelope bit back her smile, as usual, waiting for her older cousin to either compose herself or succumb to a fainting spell. To date, Pen had yet to see an actual faint. Then again, there was usually medicinal brandy nearby to come to her rescue. Pen thought perhaps she should go down to the staff area and find some of this free-flowing illegal pumpkin pie alcohol they supposedly had. But she had no time to indulge her cousin.

"Jane, I hate to take you away from the suite, but I need you to do some research for me while I'm out to make some inquiries. You're so good at that sort of thing. I need you to discover everything you can about the owner of this hotel, Genevieve Walton. Also look up anything you can find on Bentley Green. He's an architect. Mostly, I want to know if there's anything business-wise he is working on, but really whatever you can find about those two would be helpful."

Jane brightened at being handed a responsibility. "Of course, Miss Banks."

"Cousin, would you like me to have Leonard take you back to our apartment while I have him? I'd hate for you to stay in this suite all alone with a killer about." Pen was being perfectly manipulative, but it worked.

"That's a very good idea, Penelope. I most certainly *would* like to return to the safety of the apartment," Cousin Cordelia said, sitting up and looking indignant. "People being murdered right in their own beds, and who knows what else? When I think of how close I was to death today...." She fell back in some semblance of faint once again.

Penelope didn't bother correcting her assumptions. She was mildly relieved that her cousin would be going back to the security of their apartment where Chives could tend to her. Perhaps this would encourage her to finally settle on a new maid for them, if only to relieve him of some of the burden.

After calling for Leonard, it took him almost no time at all to arrive, being that they lived so close to the hotel. In fact, it took more time to coax Cousin Cordelia down to the lobby and into the car.

They delivered Cordelia to the apartment, listening to her protests and cautions the entire way. Penelope breathed a sigh of relief once she had the car to herself. She instructed Leonard to take her to the police station.

By now, he knew the way.

"You aren't in trouble again are you?" he asked with a grin as he drove.

"No, I've just somehow embroiled myself in yet another murder," she said airily. "I have to help clear a waiter's name this time."

"A friend to the working man, you are, Miss Banks. Just happy to do my part to help."

Penelope laughed as he drove. It didn't take him long to get to the 10A precinct. By now her face was familiar enough, perhaps even notorious among those who worked there.

The sergeant at the front desk visibly sighed when he saw her enter. "Miss Banks, how can I help you?" he asked in a resigned voice.

"Not to worry, I'm simply here to pick up the young man who has been an overnight guest of yours. Gary Garret?"

He studied her, no doubt wondering if she was some sort of accomplice. "He'll finish being processed soon. Feel free to come back."

"Or I can just sit here and wait?" she said with a smile.

He tightened his lips with displeasure but didn't say anything more.

While sitting down to wait, Pen pondered all of the

remaining suspects. Who might have killed both Jiro and Mandy? They had to be connected, but had the same person committed both murders?

Was Mandy's visit to Bentley something more than just a late-night tryst? Maybe Darlene had killed her in a jealous rage? Or had Bentley killed Mandy because of something to do with Jiro?

Perhaps Betty and Bobby Paxton had committed both crimes together, something related to Betty's involvement with Jiro. It was obvious Betty was hiding something.

Zounds, the possibilities seemed endless.

Rosie had hinted that Mandy was a young woman who knew how to discover people's secrets. What secrets had led to her death?

"Miss Banks?" a familiar voice said.

Penelope snapped her attention to the area behind the sergeant where Gary was exiting. He looked a sad state, with his hair no longer combed and his clothes wrinkled. He stared at her with a crooked grin of disbelief.

"What are you doing here?"

"I've come to offer you a ride home, or wherever it is you need to go."

He studied her for a moment, then smiled and shrugged. "Thanks, I guess."

Penelope rose and walked with him outside. When he saw Leonard open the door for them his eyes narrowed and he gave her a curious look, no doubt wondering what he had done to receive such special treatment.

"We can talk about it inside. Don't worry I'm here to help you."

"Is that so?" he said uncertainly, but he entered the car anyway.

"That is so," Penelope said as she followed him inside.

Leonard got in behind the wheel and started the car. Gary gave him an address on the Lower West Side which would give them plenty of time in the car together.

"I should tell you that Mandy has been murdered as well," Penelope said in a solemn tone.

Gary's eyes widened in surprise and he fell back in his seat to absorb that.

"I can only assume it had to do with Jiro Ishida's death. Can you think of any reason why someone would want her dead? Was there a connection between her and Mr. Ishida?"

Gary shook his head and shrugged, still in shock. "I mean she was sly as a fox; knew how to get what she wanted. Still, I can't see that as a reason why someone would want her dead."

"What is it she whispered to you to get you to leave the card game?" Penelope knew what Mandy had told Detective Prescott, and she wanted to see if it matched with what Gary told her now.

Gary seemed to still be in a daze at the news of her murder. He stared ahead at the back of the seat in front of him with his brow furrowed.

"Gary?"

He started and turned to her with an apologetic smile. "I'm sorry, I guess I'm just still in shock at all these people being murdered and whatnot. It was bad enough havin' one pinned on me. Mandy? She just said that Sam wanted to meet me on the roof. He's a good friend, so I went straight up, figuring he had some problem or something he needed help with.

"That's the only reason I was up there in the first place. All's I know is Sam wasn't waiting for me up on that roof. I get up there and I saw Mr. Ishida half in that pond, so my first thought was that I gotta help him, right? I rush over and pull him out—you have no idea how heavy a dead body is. Anyway, it was a struggle and I guess that's when my button came off in the pond." He gave Penelope a grim smile. "No good deed, huh?"

"So do you think it was a ploy by Mandy to get you to the roof?"

Again, he shrugged. "Knowing Mandy, it coulda been. We weren't all that close. In fact, I think she resented the connections I had."

"I understand she didn't have many friends among the staff?"

"I suppose you could say that. But I can't imagine any of them killing her."

"Can you think of why she would use Sam to get you to the roof?"

"He didn't kill Mr. Ishida if that's what you're thinking. I doubt he killed Mandy either."

"I'm not claiming that, I just want to know what was between you and Sam, and how Mandy comes into it. Mostly I'm trying to figure out if you were just a convenient frame-up, or if somebody had it in for you in particular."

He nodded with understanding. Then, he considered Penelope for a moment before speaking. "Me and Sam, we sometimes...*worked* together, you might say. He has connections. I have connections. Often the two coincide. But with this hotel, it got a little...problematic."

"Problematic how?"

"Before becoming a waiter I worked at the hotel as it was being built and decorated. Just another hired hand during construction. But work like that gives you access to any, er, *surplus* that may be lying around."

"Surplus?" Pen said in a sardonic tone.

"I probably shouldn't say too much."

"Gary, you can stop treating me like I'm your headmistress. The only thing I care about here is the murderers. I don't care about whatever side business you had going on."

He chuckled softly, then nodded and continued. "It gave me access to some pretty swanky items like silk fabric, marble, plates, glasses, vases, things like that. You know, stuff that nobody would necessarily miss if you took a little off the top. There's a market for anything and everything. Sam and me, we had an unspoken deal; nothing firm, mind you. But then I had a buyer willing to pay more than Sam was offering for the whole lot of it. Sam wasn't too happy about it, but he never thought I was trying to chisel him. He understood it was just business. That's why last night..." Gary gave Penelope a quick apologetic look.

Penelope's mouth curled. "You thought I would be an easy mark at the card game, didn't you?"

He grinned and shrugged.

"I imagine he was even more upset after losing so much," she suggested.

Gary firmly shook his head. "No, it wasn't like that. Like I said he understood it was business. We both did. Besides, he told me that night he had some kind of thing he was working on, something that might more than make up for all the hotel stuff he didn't get from me."

"But you have no idea what it was?" Pen asked, getting intrigued.

"No, but the way he said it made me think it was..."

"Not copacetic?"

He nodded. "But he's no murderer, Miss Banks, I can tell you that much."

"All the same, the detectives know that Mandy used his name to lure you to that roof, so he *is* involved. And now no one can find him. It doesn't look good. You know how the police can be, they'll target him first. Certainly before any wealthy, white guests of the Grand Opal Hotel."

Gary frowned. "I have no idea where he might be, honestly. If Sam wants to disappear, it would be easy for him. Hell, he could be halfway down to Georgia, back with his folks for all I know. Even the other members of the band probably wouldn't be able to tell you where he might be. Or at least if they did know, they'd play dumb."

Georgia. That was an interesting one, particularly with regard to certain guests of the Grand Opal Hotel. But it didn't necessarily mean anything. Pen had spent enough time in Harlem to know that most of the residents had ties to Georgia.

Besides, she suspected that any man proudly named after "the great general himself" was unlikely to be buddies with someone like Sam.

Penelope decided to move on to a new topic.

"Can you think of any reason why someone would want this case hushed up? I'm pretty sure Mr. Ishida was murdered, though not by you of course."

Gary looked genuinely surprised. "I have no idea, but I can't say I'm all that upset about it."

"Understandable. Do you think it could have been one of your connections, doing you a favor?"

He coughed out a laugh. "That's the kind of thing *friends* do, or perhaps blackmailers. My connections are strictly business, tit for tat. They wouldn't have stuck their neck out like this for me. Frankly, I'm surprised to see you helping me out. Thanks for that, Miss Banks."

She smiled. "I just want to see justice served."

"If it means me not ending up in jail again, so do I. What else do you need from me?"

"You said you worked on the hotel, did that include the gardens?"

"Naturally. A serf is a serf, after all."

"Including working with the bonsai trees?"

"Every part of that garden has a bit of yours truly involved with it."

"Did you notice anything interesting about the azalea tree, the one with the pink flowers? Or did anyone have a particular interest in it?"

His brow rose in thought. "Well as far as who was interested in it, I suppose only Mr. Ishida and Mr. Dickens. But they were focused on *everything* about that garden, obsessed even. Wanted everything to be perfect. As for that tree in particular? Yeah, I remember that one. I knew to stay well away from it, lessen I came away smelling like a French prostitute."

"How so?"

"It had a pretty strong scent, at least when they first unboxed it."

"Like it was rotting?"

"No, more like flowers. Which I guess made sense since the tree had flowers on it."

That conflicted with what Hubert Combs had said. If that kind of azalea tree didn't have a scent, why did it smell like flowers? Maybe this was a different species of azalea? And why did it transition to smelling like rot by the time the party started?

"Did it look like the same tree the night of the party? Do you think anyone could have maybe switched trees?"

He gave her a bewildered look. "I assume it was the same one. Like I said, I pretty much stayed away from it."

"Right." It was probably too much to ask that he'd be able to tell the difference anyway.

"One last thing," she said, then paused before continuing. "I saw you and Jiro talking at the party. Was he asking you for something?"

"Yeah, it was strange. He asked what kind of connections I had when it came to helping people disappear."

"As in *zotzed*?" Pen asked in surprise. She had learned quite a few colorful terms for murder over the past several years.

Gary chuckled and shook his head. "No, I mean like if someone wanted to not be found by anyone. New name, new address, stuff like that."

"Really?" Penelope said, pondering that. "So Jiro wanted to disappear?"

"I guess so. He didn't say, he just asked about it, particularly how soon I could make it happen and how much it would cost."

"Can you do something like that?"

Gary grinned. "I may know a guy who knows a guy. He could make it happen."

Penelope studied him with an amused look. "Is it true what you said about getting into the White House?"

"Like I said I know a guy who knows a guy. I make friends everywhere I can. I mean, look at me. This morning I was in a jail cell, now I'm getting chauffeured back to my apartment in style."

Penelope laughed softly. He certainly had a point.

"I imagine something like what Jiro wanted wouldn't be cheap?"

"You're telling me, doll."

"At least now I see why he was upset about not getting paid."

Penelope considered everything as they continued to drive.

MURDER IN THE GARDENS

If Jiro wanted something like that, and from the sound of it wanted it soon, he might have been desperate. Desperate enough to cause trouble even. Perhaps he had gone to Genevieve or Wendell and demanded his money, maybe even threatened them over it. That could possibly be a motive for murder. If they were selling the bonsai trees this soon after opening, there might be some financial trouble at hand.

Suddenly this case had gotten even more complicated.

The big question was *why* did Jiro want to disappear? Was he in some kind of trouble? That might have explained his murder. Whoever he was worried about may have finally caught up with him.

CHAPTER SIXTEEN

"I really do wish you good luck on the case, Miss Banks," Gary said as he exited the car in front of his apartment building. "I didn't know Mr. Ishida all that well but he seemed like a decent man. I hope you find whoever did this to him, and to Mandy of course."

"I'll do my best, boy-o."

Gary grinned and closed the door.

"Now, it's the long trek back to the hotel, Leonard."

"Yes ma'am," he said with a chuckle. "So, did that help at all?"

"As far as getting closer to who killed either of them, not all that much," she confessed. "Still, I'm not completely out of avenues to explore."

It was almost dusk by the time the car made it through the throng of traffic and arrived at the Grand Opal Hotel. The lobby still had a lingering police presence. There were also still a few members of the press outside hoping to catch a story. Penelope imagined Mr. Dickens wasn't too happy about that.

Hopefully, Jane had some information for her by now.

The simple task of collecting Gary and taking them all the way downtown to his apartment and back here again had eaten the remainder of the afternoon. Pen was pleased to see that Jane was in fact back from her mission.

"Good evening, Miss Banks," she said brightly. "I'm afraid the research area of the library closes at five, but I did try to learn as much as I could."

Penelope smiled appreciatively and fell next to her on the sofa feeling her weariness setting in. "Spill the goods, doll."

"As far as Miss Walton, most of the information I gathered from newspapers was of course about this hotel. But she has an interesting history. I can see why she chose Japanese as a theme. Her father was a Minister to Japan for ten years. She lived there with him during that time, from age ten to twenty. So I imagine she developed a fondness for the country."

"Apparently," Penelope agreed. If her father was a minister to Japan that meant he had political influence and no doubt *some* money, but enough to build a hotel? Enough to hush up a murder case? It was something to consider.

"Did you learn anything about her finances? How she funded this hotel?"

Jane frowned and studied her handy notepad. "The only thing I learned was that there were private investors involved."

So no traditional financing. Interesting.

"In other words, people who expect a return on their investment."

Jane simply shrugged.

"And what did you learn about Bentley Green?"

Jane started with the business side of things.

"His firm just won a bid to work on several new luxury hotels for the Sinclair family throughout America."

"And I imagine they might have welcomed their own Japanese gardens? After all, both the Ritz and the Astor hotels have them, and of course now the Grand Opal. They are quite a thing these days."

"I confess I did have a quick peek before I left to start my research," Jane said, coloring furiously at her little act of mischief. "It is lovely, different from any garden I've ever seen. I can see why they're so popular."

"It is, popular enough for murder, unfortunately. What else did you learn about Bentley?"

"Well," Jane began, pausing to take a breath. "There's a history of his involvement with the law, though I couldn't get a firm grasp on it. Most of it was dismissed or hushed up or paid for with a fine. But apparently he likes to throw notorious parties. Why they are notorious, I'm not sure. I confess that some of my research came from the *New York Tattle*."

They had a history with that gossip sheet.

"Just because it's the worst sort of rag doesn't mean it publishes lies...*necessarily*," Penelope added. She had learned that often where there was smoke, there was definitely fire.

With what little time Jane had been given, she had produced a nice bit of work, and she congratulated her associate.

"So, Genevieve Walton had private investors that are no doubt hoping to make quick money. But surely people who invest in a hotel realize it will take time to recoup their financial gain? The hotel has only just opened, after all. And what would that have to do with the murder of Jiro?

"As for Bentley Green, I now understand why he's here.

He was probably hoping to poach Jiro now that his work here was done. If he could secure the best Japanese garden designer in New York, if not the country, that would have been a huge boon with regard to these hotels he was building."

"So why kill him?" Jane asked.

"Good point. Still, that doesn't necessarily absolve him of Mandy's murder. Either way, it seems like both people are *less* likely suspects than they were before."

"I'm sorry I couldn't get more information for you, Miss Banks. I only had a few hours to do the research," Jane said, misreading her response.

Penelope shot her a reassuring smile. "No, no you did wonderful research, as usual, Jane. I just realized I'm going to have to investigate further, which means inviting myself to dinner with someone I'm not particularly interested in dining with."

"Detective Prescott?" Jane said, giving her an admonishing look. Jane adored him, and probably already had Pen married to him in her head.

Penelope laughed. "Oh Jane, you could give Cupid himself some hearty competition. No, no, I mean my father."

"Oh, well, I'm sure he'd love to have dinner with you, you are his daughter after all."

"That's how I know it will be miserable. But alas, such is this occupation. It can get rather messy. *You* can at least enjoy your night. The second bedroom is all yours, Jane, now that my poor cousin has vacated it. Order room service and luxuriate in it to your heart's content."

"Really? Thank you, Miss Banks!"

"But before that, one final request. I need you to send a telegram. Quite urgently."

MURDER IN THE GARDENS

Pen wasn't about to let the night go completely to waste.

At promptly eight o'clock that night Penelope arrived at the mansion further up 5th Ave that she had grown up in. The last time she had had dinner here with her father she had been on the cusp of learning that she was going to be a millionaire, though via unfortunate means.

The door was opened by the butler she had also grown up with.

"Good evening, Coleman," she greeted warmly.

"Good evening, Miss Penelope," he said in his stately manner, still giving that slight nod to familiarity by using her first name.

As always Penelope marveled at the life-sized painting in the foyer of her mother who had died during the Great Influenza. Penelope had learned so many secrets about her mother in the past several months, but most of it had only made her more of a mystery. All Pen knew was that Juliette Williams had been a performer, estranged from her family in San Francisco. It was apparently a family that she had a very good reason to be estranged from after she'd met Reginald Banks, who was almost the exact opposite of her. Penelope wasn't quite sure she entirely trusted only her father's word on the matter. At some point, she would delve deeper into it, but she was somewhat worried about what she might find.

She dismissed the painting and followed Coleman into the dining room where her father was already seated. Just seeing him and his stern demeanor made Penelope long for the days when she could make a cocktail for herself before she sat down with him, or at least sip on wine through dinner. As it was, she requested a ginger ale when Coleman asked.

"Good evening father," she said cheerily as she sat down next to where he was situated at the head of the table.

"Should I be worried or pleased?" he said by way of a greeting. "I assume that you have news to tell me or something to inquire of me."

"Can't a daughter simply have dinner with her father?" Penelope asked innocently.

He returned a dry look, not deigning to answer that question, which he obviously didn't find amusing.

"Oh very well," Penelope said. "Yes, I did have something to ask of you. I was wondering how much you knew about the Grand Opal Hotel, specifically the owner, Genevieve Walton?"

Her father worked in investment and finance. She knew he had an encyclopedic knowledge of anything related to business, so he would probably know more than anyone about the financing behind the hotel.

"A frivolous endeavor," he said instantly.

"Really? But it's so lovely. I've been staying there this weekend and it's exquisite. The attention to detail is impressive and the garden on the roof is the most gorgeous I've ever seen. It'll be the envy of every other hotel. Even the Ritz just a block away should be worried, I would think."

Her father exhaled a laugh. "I don't think the people at the Ritz will be shaking in their boots, Penelope. That silly woman had very little money to begin with, and she somehow cajoled even more silly minds into pouring their money into that hotel. It may be very fine and all, but that's of little concern when it comes to the bottom line. Her fascination with the Orient will be her downfall. These gardens that are popping up everywhere are a fad. Never put your money into fads, Penelope. Tried and true is the only way."

"So you think the hotel will fail?"

"More than likely it'll be purchased for a song by some more prudent investor. She'll be lucky if she gets whatever she put into it, which to my understanding is everything she has. Further proof women and business don't mix."

Penelope glared at him.

"Don't you start. There's a reason you don't see women on Wall Street. Their disposition is best suited for the hearth and home." He eyed her speculatively. "Though some manage to seep through the cracks."

"And some manage to build an entire hotel," Pen said, feeling her hackles rise as usual when she was with her father.

"We'll see how that works out for her. Though, I imagine for Miss Walton the loss of her vanity project will be the bigger disappointment than any financial loss."

That had Penelope ignoring her instant desire to counter her father in favor of the case she was working on. This was certainly interesting news. So Miss Walton was in more of a financially precarious condition than Penelope thought.

"Speaking of hotels, I hear the Sinclairs are building a line of them? They've supposedly hired Bentley Green to design them? He's been staying at the Grand Opal Hotel as well, no doubt to latch on to this supposed *fad* in gardens for their hotels."

Her father's brow rose in alarm. "I certainly hope you haven't been associating with that man."

Pen couldn't help inserting a bit of devilishness into this evening.

"He does happen to occupy the suite across from me," she replied with a mischievous smile.

Her father scowled, realizing she was teasing him. "If he keeps up with his degenerate lifestyle, he'll soon go the way of his mentor. Stanford was a brilliant architect, but an unabashed scoundrel. If you ask me, being shot was too good for him, considering what he did."

It didn't surprise Pen that her father disapproved of Bentley's womanizing ways. He was the bluest of bluenoses.

"As it turns out Bentley might be involved in a murder himself. One of the maids at the hotel, who I know for a fact he was associating with, was murdered."

At the mention of murder, her father scowled again. "What have you been involving yourself with, Penelope?"

"I can't help it if people get murdered around me. But it was fortunate I was there. I can help solve the case."

Her father exhaled explosively. "I knew it! I just *knew* it! Once again, you're meddling in things that don't concern you. Any other daughter would be married with children by now, but I have been cursed with one who thinks she is the next Sherlock Holmes."

"What did you expect when you cut me off? I had to learn to survive on my own."

"Yes, you did," he grumbled unhappily.

Penelope tilted her head and considered him as something occurred to her. "You thought I would come running back home, didn't you?"

"I *thought* you would see reason. I suppose that's my fault for underestimating you."

"You always have."

"No, I haven't, if I'm being honest with myself. You've turned out exactly as I expected. I should have known with that mind of yours you'd get involved in something problematic, all the better to put it to meddlesome use. Involving yourself in an occupation that is best left for men."

"Feminism is becoming more and more attractive," Penelope mused, knowing perfectly well she was stirring the pot.

Sure enough her father exhaled once again, this time in exasperation. "I do wish you would keep these radical thoughts to yourself. I have no interest in hearing about feminism or any other anarchist ideas."

"I'm pretty sure those are two different ideologies," she said, then tilted her head to the side in thought. "Well, there *might* be some crossover."

"Perhaps we could simply enjoy dinner without you bringing up these newfangled notions that you've learned in your *occupation*. My secretary tells me you brought a man with you when you came to visit me at my office several weeks ago. A fellow with a scar."

"Richard Prescott? You might say we are...associates."

"Associates or something more?" He studied her with a keen gaze.

"Well, I *have* been throwing myself at him like a perfect harlot, but he's been too much of a gentleman thus far to ravish me in the way I'd hoped he would."

By now her father was used to her teasing him and he didn't take the bait. He simply gave her another scowl before he continued. "I'm quite resistant to your vulgarity by now, Penelope."

"A shame, I had hoped there was still a chance to corrupt you."

He ignored that. "He's a detective I understand? Did he get the scar in the line of duty?"

"You could say that. He was in the Great War. I'm

pretty sure he flew planes."

"Hmmm," her father said, looking impressed. "Well, at least he's a patriot, not that I saw any reason for us to involve ourselves in that nonsense. A bunch of inbred monarchs having a family squabble and seeing fit to involve the whole world in it. Still, good on him for doing his part all the same. Although, I'm not sure how I feel about you involving yourself with a detective. Nothing against the profession of course, but don't you think you should be with someone of your own status?"

"What makes you think he isn't of my status? He graduated from Princeton, and he knows quite a bit about art. In fact, he knows quite a bit about a lot of things." Penelope furrowed her brow in thought. Now that she had said it, there were several clues that made her think that Richard Prescott hadn't necessarily grown up in a working-class background.

"Perhaps next time you decide I'm *worthy* of your time you can bring him by. I'd be curious to meet him."

"Are you sure you'd lower yourself to having dinner with someone who isn't of your status?"

"I'm not a snob, Penelope. Worrying about my daughter's future and who she plans on spending it with is a father's prerogative. I'm allowed to be biased when it comes to that."

"Where was all this prejudice when Clifford Stokes was having an affair with Constance?" Pen said in a testy voice.

"In retrospect, I was wrong about that."

Penelope was astonished that he was admitting it.

"*However*, in all fairness, that wedding, in fact, that whole relationship was the final straw after years of you being perfectly frivolous with your life. I thought perhaps the marriage, as problematic as it was, would tame you of your wanton ways. Dropping out of college. Parties every night. Running off to Spain for a month? Deciding to take up *snooker*?

"Yes, when I cut you off, I was hoping that you would finally find some direction, maybe even go back to college and find a more serious man to settle down with. Instead, I have," he waved his hand in her direction, "*this*."

"Not to worry father, *this* is probably happier and more focused than she's ever been in life. I have a career that I very much enjoy, and a wonderful group of friends and associates who often help me in my occupation."

"And a father you only come to when you need information for this *occupation* of yours."

"You did keep me from going to prison last time, so you can consider your fatherly duties more than satisfied."

"Am I keeping you from prison this time?"

"Don't fret, I'm not a suspect in this case. There are quite a few other people on that list."

"Well, I suppose that's a relief."

Penelope was set to argue further, but she remembered why she was here. In fact, something now came back to her. "Do you know anything about Burnside Development? Are they one of the investors in the Grand Opal Hotel?"

Her father seemed surprised at the shift in topics. However, they had moved on to one that was his forte, and he immediately transitioned into a focus on business.

"Burnside Development? I should think not. They're far too established to involve themselves in something like that risky enterprise. Besides, they only handle residential properties, these new luxury apartment buildings going up everywhere, tarnishing the footprint of the city."

"But it's a similar industry, isn't it? Hotels and apartments?"

Her father gave her a patient smile. "You have a lot to learn about business, Penelope. There is a significant difference between the rental property business and the hospitality business. Burnside builds and holds onto apartment buildings, making their money by collecting rents, mostly from those with a high income. No tenement buildings for them, thank you very much."

Penelope pondered that. If Burnside Development wasn't involved in the Grand Opal Hotel, why had Wendell Dickens had correspondence from them? Perhaps he was thinking of moving on to rental property management. Maybe he saw the sinking ship that the hotel was becoming and, like a rat, was scurrying away as quickly as he could for safer, drier land.

"I, myself, don't understand it. Why the wealthy are moving into apartments and away from stately mansions like this is beyond me."

"There are more people moving to New York every day. Space is a shrinking commodity, why not build up?"

Her father shook his head in wonder. "There's a lot of shady dealings going on if you ask me. It's all moving too fast for my comfort."

Something about that sparked a note in Penelope's head. Shady dealings—in other words, not copacetic. It seemed Jiro might have been involved in something sinister, considering his request of Gary. Why else would he want to disappear? And Mandy was known to be somewhat shady herself. Maybe this deal Sam had told Gary about was connected. She needed to talk to him more than ever, certainly before the police got to him.

And Penelope already knew exactly how to do that. She wasn't without her own shady dealings.

CHAPTER SEVENTEEN

Penelope's dinner with her father hadn't been as terrible as she had predicted. They had eventually moved on to safer fare in terms of conversation, which meant he had bored her to tears with the latest in business. She came away learning that Sears Robuck had finally opened their first retail store in Chicago, moving them into the modern era, according to him. Penelope doubted the convenience of ordering something and having it delivered right to your front door would ever disappear. There was also some corporation that had just formed, named Chrysler that was now making luxury cars.

While none of it was of much interest to Pen, this career of hers had taught her that she needed to broaden her scope of knowledge. Thus, she filed it all away just the same for future use.

Now, she was headed to the Peacock Club. This late hour of the night, even on a Sunday, it was just getting lively. She had invited her friend Benny Davenport to join her to meet with Lucille "Lulu" Simmons at the club. Thankfully, Lulu wasn't working tonight. Since the Peacock

Club was integrated, unlike places like the Cotton Club, it meant she could sit with them and drink.

More importantly, Penelope could beseech her friends for help with this case.

She sat at her favorite table, which she was certain Lulu had made sure was reserved for them. As she took her seat, Penelope saw her at another table with Tommy Callahan. He was the favorite young henchman of one of New York's most notorious gang bosses, Mr. Jack Sweeney. The two of them were in a heated conversation over something and Lulu looked perfectly ready to end it. Pen hoped she wasn't in trouble, as Mr. Sweeney had a majority stake in the Peacock Club. Lulu caught Penelope's eyes and smiled from across the club. She gave one last parting word to Tommy which had him go quiet in a sullen manner, then she walked over.

"Is everything alright?" Penelope asked.

"Dandy as candy, darling," Lulu said easily as she sat down. "Just Tommy trying to overstep his control, as usual."

Penelope left that one alone. Neither of them was a saint, and frankly, neither was Pen herself. She knew enough about what went on in places like this to know that whatever business they were involved in was none of hers, and she had no desire to make it so.

"So you received my message?"

"I did," Lulu said noncommittally. Her catlike eyes narrowed as she studied Penelope.

The telegram that Penelope had Jane send asked Lulu if she knew where Sam Trebant might be hiding out and if she could finagle a way of getting Penelope in touch with him. She was glad she hadn't underestimated Lulu's resourcefulness. But why was she being coy now?

"And?" Penelope asked slightly exasperated.

"And what?"

"Zounds! At least now I see why Tommy always gets so frustrated with you. You really do like making people work for it, don't you?"

Lulu laughed and sipped her champagne. After pulling the glass away she studied Penelope once again. "I'm just curious about what you're after."

"Justice? The truth?"

"People have different definitions of justice," she said in a slightly resentful tone.

"Don't be like that Lulu, you know me. Were you able to get in touch with Sam or not? I would like to think he'd rather talk to me than the police."

"Not if you're going to go running your mouth to your little detective friend."

"He's not my *little detective friend*," Penelope said her face getting warm. "And if anything, Sam should be happy if I go and tell that *little detective* because *he* would at least treat him fairly."

Lulu just hummed and sipped her champagne.

"I only care about the murders, Lulu. Whatever side business he has going on isn't of concern to me. Heaven knows I'm the last person on earth who should judge." As if to stress the point Pen lifted her own glass of champagne and sipped. "I suspect he didn't kill Jiro or Mandy, but him hiding this way doesn't make him look good. You know how the police are."

"Just because they can't find him doesn't mean that he's necessarily hiding."

"Alright, but at least warn him that the longer this goes on the antsier they're going to become. They like closing cases quickly, especially murders. My only motivation is to get some answers from him, like why Mandy used his name to lure Gary to the roof, and what deal it is he had going on that night, that's all."

"I'll make sure he gets your message."

Penelope realized that's as much as she could hope for. She saw Benny come into the club and waved him toward their table.

"Lulu, looking divine as ever," he said pursing his lips at her when he arrived.

"The same could be said of you, darling," Lulu tossed right back.

Benny sat down between them. "And Pen, I see we have another case we're working on. I heard all about it. Was it terribly tragic?"

"Death is always tragic, Benny, which is why I've come to ask the two of you for help."

Benny poured himself a glass of champagne from the bottle. "I'm not sure what I have to offer, dove. My only interest in gardening is whether or not it's pleasing to the eye. I have a preference for colorful flowers."

"Yes, we know, Benny," Lulu said with a smirk.

He pursed his lips at her again, then turned back to Penelope. "Is the hotel as magnificent as they say?"

"That's neither here nor there. You might find out for yourself if this case ever gets solved," she hinted.

"So what is it you want of me, dove?"

"Bentley Green."

That name was apparently notorious enough for both of them to sit up straighter with renewed interest.

Benny considered Penelope. "I suppose at twenty-four you're not *terribly* old for his preferred taste. The better question is…why?" He added with an exaggeratedly bewildered look. "You certainly don't need the money, and you could do so much better, Pen."

Penelope wrinkled her nose with distaste. "I'm not interested in him for that reason, I just want to know what you know about him. Specifically any shady dealings he might be involved in?"

"His architectural endeavors are of no interest to me; I prefer the classical structures. Nothing like a good, sturdy column."

He and Lulu giggled at that.

"If you two are done acting like children, perhaps you can tell me more about something that may help me solve a murder?"

"Yes of course, Pen. Bentley Green, his…extracurricular pursuits? *That* is the stuff of ribald delight."

"How specifically?"

"Other than the cliché of younger women—all above age mind you; he certainly learned his lesson after Stanford—certain…substances are procured for guests at his infamous parties."

"Parties?" Perhaps this was what Jane had touched upon in her research.

"Very exclusive, limited to powerful, influential men like himself, and their bright young partners of course. The kind of men who, say for example, can't be caught visiting one of our cities' opium establishments?"

"*Opium?*"

"He apparently has his own connection and everything. Usually, one has to venture out for that sort of thing, not that I ever indulge."

All very scandalous, but Pen still wasn't sure how it applied to this case. Had Jiro been selling opium? If so, why? He had a brilliant career that was just reaching popularity. Surely he hadn't been that desperate for money?

She decided to ask Benny about some of the other occupants of the hotel, hoping he might know some gossip about them as well.

"Do you know a golfer named Bobby Paxton?"

Benny gave her a deadpan look. "You lost me the moment you said golf, Pen. I have no interest in sports and golf is the dullest of them all."

"What about a man named Hubert Combs?"

At that name, Benny twisted his lips with pleasure. "Oh yes, Mr. Combs, there's a name that's quite familiar. Let's just say Hubert and I frequent many of the same...establishments." He arched one eyebrow meaningfully.

Penelope mentally revisited Hubert's affect, and that seemed to fit. Again, she had no idea how it would connect to this murder. All it told her was that he definitely wouldn't have had any interest in Mandy's charms.

"What about Genevieve Walton?"

"Not quite as wealthy as she puts on. I've heard the financing of that hotel is rather unscrupulous."

"You mean loan sharking?" Penelope's brow rose in surprise.

"Of a sort, I suppose. There were rumors about why her father spent so long as a diplomat in Japan. He apparently had his own business dealings going on in that country. He came back relatively wealthy, certainly much wealthier than he was when he was sent there. Now, his daughter, after a life of living extravagantly has decided to pour the final amount into this swan song of a hotel."

"I don't suppose you know anything about Jiro Ishida?"

"Only that the *girls* won't stop talking about him. I swear the entire city will be filled with Japanese gardens before the decade is over. Though, I suppose that's no longer the case now," he added in a droll tone.

"I wish you would take these things seriously, Benny.

I'm trying to find out who killed these two people before the police decide to either ignore this case, or worse, pin it on a convenient target. After all, it isn't as though the murder of a Japanese man or a maid would be as important to them as, say, yours or mine."

Lulu had been studying Penelope, and she finally set her glass down.

"Alright, Pen, come with me."

Penelope shifted her attention. "Where to?"

"You want to talk to Sam? Come with me."

"He's been here the whole time?"

"Is it me you're interrogating, now? Come on, Pen."

Penelope quickly set her drink down and rose from her seat. She followed Lulu into the back hallway. They exited out of the back door into the alleyway and Lulu led her a few doors down.

"Now, before I do this, you *never* heard of this place."

"What *is* this place?" Penelope asked, suddenly curious.

"You folks have your places to hide away, and we have ours. This is one of them."

"And I've never heard of it," Pen assured her with a grin.

Lulu smiled and knocked on the door. After a moment Pen heard some noise on the other side.

"Who is it?"

"It's Lulu, I have Penelope Banks with me."

The door opened a crack, and Pen recognized the face of Sam peeking out. He narrowed his eyes at her then cast a questioning glance toward Lulu.

"It's fine Sam. I think she really wants to help."

"I do," Penelope insisted.

He scowled for a moment, then opened the door for them. It led to the hallway of an apartment building. He opened the first door on their right and they entered a tiny, barely furnished apartment. Without a word, he sank into a chair and gestured for them to sit on the shabby couch.

"I just want to know what happened that night, is all. Do you know why Mandy used your name to get Gary up to the roof?"

Another scowl came to his face. "It took me all of one night of working at that dang hotel to know that girl was trouble. I didn't even need to hear the rumors from everyone else."

"But why target you specifically? Or was it Gary that she was targeting?"

"Probably both of us. Gary and I were...associates of a sort." He studied Penelope to see her reaction to that. She gave him a dryly amused look. He relaxed and continued. "Gary knows how to make connections, same as me. That boy could get into any job. You know he worked construction on that Lincoln Memorial down in D.C.? Well, from there he went straight to delivering vegetables to the White House. Says he met the president himself, but I doubt that." Sam chuckled.

Pen smiled remembering his comment in the elevator. But she wanted to move on.

"And Mandy?"

"That one? What I *can* tell you is she was getting mixed up in some dark business. I don't think even she realized how dangerous it was. Though, I guess maybe she learned the hard way, didn't she?"

"Like what?"

"Opium."

Penelope and Lulu looked at each other. Something was finally connecting in this case.

"How do you know she was involved in that?"

"Because she asked me about it. She probably thought because of who I was, I knew where she could get some," he said with a look of disgust on his face.

"So she wanted to *buy* it?" Penelope confirmed.

"She asked me if I knew someone who sold it." He leaned in and gave Penelope a direct look. "*Everyone* knows not to mess with that business. First of all, the police? They don't look too kindly on that stuff. You pay 'em enough they'll look the other way when it comes to bootleg booze and gambling. Something like opium, they come down hard. You need big money, big influence, or a big enough scare to keep them away. And I ain't got none of that. They even have these dogs that can smell the stuff. But that's not even the biggest concern. There's only one group in town that deals in that business, and I definitely don't mess with the Tong gangs." He jerked his chin at Lulu. "Even your Tommy-boy ain't got nothing on them."

"He's not *my* Tommy boy," Lulu said in a terse voice.

Sam's mouth hitched into a half-smile, and he rolled his eyes back to Penelope. "I'd say that's where, why, and how Mandy got herself bumped. Yeah, I heard about her murder. I could have told her, messing with that stuff, it don't end well."

"She went to see Bentley Green that night, and I just found out that he has a connection to that business. Maybe she was trying to get some as a way to ingratiate herself to him? She told me she soon wouldn't have to worry about money. I have to assume this was what she was talking about."

"Why would he need her if he already had his own connections?" Lulu posed.

Penelope bit her lip in thought. "I don't know. Maybe

she was trying to start her own business? Maybe his connections had fallen through?"

"Ambitious girl," she hummed.

"So I've been told."

"Perhaps it didn't go exactly according to plan and *Bentley Green* killed her for it," Sam said meaningfully.

"Perhaps," Penelope echoed, but she studied him. "Gary said that you had a big deal going on that night. What was it?"

He worked his jaw to the side, not answering at first.

"If you want me to help you, I need to know the facts. I don't care if what you were involved with was illegal, I only care about the murders and who committed them."

He stared at her for a moment, then nodded. "When you're a member of the band, you overhear a lot of things people don't think you can hear. That golfer's wife? I heard some of the conversation between her and Mr. Ishida. Something involving a lot of money—something about it being *unethical* money. They planned to meet back on the roof later that evening to discuss it after the party when no one was around. I decided to go up and learn more, maybe get a cut of the deal myself.

"I took the staff elevator up forgetting how long that dang thing takes. I had meant to get there before they were supposed to meet, but that didn't work out. Anyway, I get up there and I see that golfer's wife handling that man's body. I figured maybe she didn't like how the conversation went and tried to drown him or something. All I knew was he was definitely dead and I wasn't going to be the one to stick around to investigate why or how. I went right back down, taking the stairs this time, and left the building as quickly as I could."

"She was handling the body?" Pen asked.

MURDER IN THE GARDENS

"Leaning right over the water and everything."

Betty certainly hadn't mentioned that. It seemed she had more involvement with Jiro's body than she had let on. Still, thinking back to that slight woman, Pen couldn't even imagine her drowning Mr. Ishida on her own. He had been fairly well-built. But her along with someone else, for instance Mandy...

"Did you see anything else while you were up there?"

He shook his head, then suddenly stopped. "Actually, there was a trail of dirt on the stairs along the way."

"Dirt?"

"Yeah. Dirt and water drops." He nodded "On the walkway leading to the door and in the stairwell. I figure it came from that empty stand where all them small trees were."

Penelope hadn't seen any dirt or water when she went up the stairwell. So whoever had cleaned up the blood from Jiro's head wound had also cleaned up that dirt and water, essentially any evidence of them stealing that tree or killing Jiro. It would have to have been after Betty and Sam had been up on the roof—if neither of them was the culprit.

But Sam was being awfully forthcoming about everything. He hadn't needed to admit to being up on the roof at all, but he did. And his story matched what Betty had said she had heard.

As for Betty, she now seemed to have a motive, or at least questionable circumstances. What was this unethical money all about? She had said there had been almost a good twenty minutes before she had made that call to alert Wendell about the body. Twenty minutes, plus however long it took him to get to the roof, was time enough to clean up the blood, dirt, and water, all to try and make Jiro's death look like an accident.

And then send Gary up to take the fall.

"So Jiro was dead and the tree was gone when you went up there. And someone took that tree right from the stand and went down the stairway to escape."

"Not all the way down though, the dirt stopped after one or two flights."

"Was it one flight or two flights?" Penelope pressed.

He coughed out a laugh. "Lady, I wasn't exactly paying too close attention to no dirt or water on the stairs at the time!"

She sighed and nodded in understanding. "So that means someone took the tree to one of the suites on either the seventeenth or sixteenth floor. Which means if Mandy was involved in this, she had help from someone on one of those floors."

"Maybe after *they* killed Mr. Ishida," Sam said, again in a meaningful voice.

"Yes, I get it, you didn't commit the murder, Sam," she said with an exasperated look. "The question is, which of the hotel occupants in those suites did?"

Despite what she had just learned about Betty, Pen's mind instantly went to Bentley. The opium connection. The fact that Mandy went straight to his room after coming to hers. It was too much of a coincidence.

But he and Darlene had checked out of the hotel before Mandy had been found dead. Pen recalled seeing her in the lobby before questioning Betty.

So who else could it have been?

CHAPTER EIGHTEEN

Despite how late she had returned to the hotel, Penelope spent the night mostly in restless sleep. After everything she'd learned last night, every potential suspect had suddenly become more sinister.

But the next morning her mind was refreshed, and she had finally put something together that might help clear at least one thing up.

Which meant she needed to talk to the Paxtons urgently.

She got dressed and exited her bedroom to find Jane in the living room. She was wearing the kimono provided in her own bedroom. It was also white with pink cherry blossoms.

"I see you're enjoying the amenities," Pen said with a grin.

"I hadn't planned on spending the night so I didn't bring a change of clothes with me," Jane said sheepishly. "I've never felt anything this luxurious."

"I suppose I'll have to buy it for you, now. Though, I

think I know a guy who knows a guy who can get me one in the black market," she added with a sardonic smile.

"I can go put on my old clothes," Jane said "What are we starting with today?"

"Applesauce," Penelope replied. "You stay right there in that robe. In fact, I insist you order some room service for breakfast. I'm going to jot out and do a little questioning based on some things that I learned last night."

"Oh, I really shouldn't, Miss Banks. Besides, your cousin did have a point about the orchids. The scent does seem to linger, particularly in the bathroom."

"Still, I can't have you wearing your old clothes, Jane. What kind of a draconian boss would I be? I'll pull out something from my own clothes for you to wear. We're about the same size." She put a hand up to stop Jane before she could protest. "I insist, and there will be no argument from you."

"Were Benny and Lulu helpful last night?"

"In their own way, as usual. I suppose we all make a grand team don't we?"

Jane laughed.

Penelope lent Jane a pretty dress in blue to match her cornflower eyes. Then she breezed out of the suite leaving her associate to enjoy a relaxed morning. Rather than wait for the elevator she took the stairs up to the seventeenth floor and knocked on the door of the Presidential Suite.

On the other side, Pen could hear some rustling and assumed that whoever was there was looking through the peephole. One moment later, the door opened a crack and Betty's face looked out, her eyes already glaring.

"I thought I told you I had nothing else to say to you. I don't care if the detective isn't with you, you can talk to our attorney as well."

MURDER IN THE GARDENS

Before she could fully close the door Penelope spoke up. "You can talk to me or you can explain to the police why your husband was trying to buy opium from Bentley Green last night. I know there's something wrong with his arm."

Betty's eyes went wide with shock, but she at least stopped trying to close the door on Pen. "How dare you make those kinds of accusations!"

"Perhaps you can clarify in the privacy of your suite rather than here in the hallway where anyone can hear." Penelope turned her head to look at the door to the Emperor Suite at the other end of the hall, then turned back to Betty. "Or...we can discuss it with the police?"

"Just let her in, darlin'," Penelope heard a man's voice call out from somewhere inside the suite. She recognized it as Bobby's.

Betty hesitated, glared at Penelope again, and then opened the door wider for her to enter.

Penelope was awed for a moment by the grandiose suite. It took up half the entire floor, which was understandable being that it was the Presidential Suite. The decor here was in cool and calming colors of blue, gray, and silver, but still with the oriental flair. She dismissed that in favor of the man resting on the couch giving her a grim look.

"What is it you've heard about me—Miss Banks, was it?"

"Yes, and I haven't *heard* anything, I'm just putting a lot of things together. Last night when you tried to raise your arm to put it around your wife you stopped halfway. I thought maybe you two were having a spousal spat. However, later that evening, after the murder, you struggled while trying to get up from the sofa. It's not exactly good for the career of a golfer to have an injured arm. Was that why you were seeking a certain type of medication, in the form

179

of opium, specifically? That *is* what you were discussing with Bentley Green, was it not? Is that why he was so angry with you?"

Bobby stared at her for a moment then breathed out a humorless laugh. "I suppose my secret's out, ain't it?"

"*Bobby*," Betty exclaimed with a look of alarm.

"I'm not telling anyone about what you say, not unless it's related to the murders. Otherwise, your secret is safe with me. I'm only interested in knowing why someone may have killed Jiro or Mandy."

"Neither of us had anything to do with either of those murders, I already told you," Betty said sitting down next to her husband.

Penelope decided to address her.

"Why was it you were really meeting with Jiro Ishida on the roof last night? Was it to get opium for your husband?"

Betty gasped in shock. "Of course not!"

Bobby took hold of her hand and squeezed then leaned in to give Penelope a dark look. "My wife has nothing to do with any of that business, Miss Banks. She's a good woman, one who absolutely sticks by my side, and wants only what's best for me. In fact, she was the one telling me not to get involved with that stuff. I know how addictive it can be, how many lives it's ruined. However, I do have my career to think about."

"You won't have much of a career if your arm is injured. No more free suites in New York. No more cash prizes from tournaments. If everyone sees how poorly you perform this week, that would be it for you. Surely a supportive wife would take that into consideration."

"Like my husband said I *abhor* that drug. So did Jiro. He would *never* have involved himself in such a thing, especially opium. He hated the association it had with people from the Asian continent. He blamed that drug in part on the prejudices that he faced in this country."

Penelope stared at her, taking note of how ardently she defended Jiro. Perhaps he wasn't involved in opium, but that didn't necessarily clear her. She had to depend on her husband's career. The idea of poverty made people do desperate things. At the very least, it tested their morals.

"So, again, why is it you were really going to the roof to meet him? And before you deny anything or lie, I have information from someone who heard your discussion with him at the party. That you were planning to do something involving money, something unethical."

Betty stared at her, eyes wide.

Bobby snapped his attention to his wife. "Honey, you didn't. Please tell me you didn't."

Penelope felt her heart beat faster. Was he accusing his wife of killing Jiro?

"If it was an accident, I'm sure the police would understand," Penelope said in a sympathetic voice, trying to coax a confession out of her.

Bobby turned to look at Penelope in confusion. "My wife didn't kill anybody. She..."

"I was trying to help Jiro get money," Betty finished for him.

"How?" Penelope asked.

Again, the couple looked at each other, some unspoken communication passing forth between them. Finally, Bobby nodded at his wife.

Betty turned to Penelope. "I was telling him how he could make money by betting against my husband in the tournament this week."

"You see, no one knows about my arm yet, Miss Banks.

At least no one up here in New York does. It's my shoulder, something in the joint that has been building for a while and just reared its ugly head with a raging fire this past week. I can struggle through all eighteen holes, but my game is going to be something awful. People are gonna notice. In fact, I secretly had money put down against myself. I suppose my wife was trying to get Jiro to do the same."

"But he was too honorable to do such a thing," Betty said. "That's how I know he wouldn't have ever been involved in something like *opium*. He was hesitant to even do something like bet against my husband's game. No matter how much he desperately needed the money."

"Do you know what he needed the money for?"

"He wanted to help his family back in Japan. His parents and his younger sister they're Japanese citizens. They had him during the period they lived here, which makes him a citizen. But the rest of them are still stuck in Japan. There's a very powerful man who wants to marry Jiro's sister, Takashi Ando. A man she has no interest in marrying. A man who could destroy them. They would be in terrible danger if she says no, so Jiro wanted to bring them here to live with him, so they'd be safe. But that horrible act Congress passed last year, it prevents anyone from any Asian country immigrating here.

"We both knew there were ways people could get papers in the black market. Something to prove that they were citizens of the United States. Unfortunately, since that act passed such a thing has been quite in demand, which means it costs a lot of money, especially for three people."

So *that's* what Jiro wanted from Gary. He hadn't been trying to escape himself, he'd wanted to help his family escape.

MURDER IN THE GARDENS

"Jiro had been hoping the money paid to him from his work on the garden for this hotel would cover it. But then that *woman* decided not to pay him. She claimed that she would only be able to pay him in a few weeks after certain things had happened. She wouldn't even let him work for someone else. He'd received a very generous offer from someone to work on a number of new gardens, but this contract had him in a chokehold with a non-compete clause. Even if he had accepted this new work, he couldn't wait that long. His family depended on him. That's why I told him about my husband's secret. How he could use it to get the money by betting a large sum."

"How do you know so much about Jiro?" Penelope still wasn't ruling out the idea that there might have been an affair going on.

Betty flashed a sad smile.

"I met Mr. Ishida a year ago when my husband had a tournament in New York. He was giving a talk at the botanical gardens about Japanese gardening and the concept of Zen. It all seemed so...peaceful. I wanted to learn more, and we got to talking. I just felt this connection with him—though nothing like what you have been insinuating," she said with a brief look of resentment at Penelope. "I considered him a friend, nothing more Miss Banks. When I returned to Georgia, we kept in touch via letters.

"When I found out about my husband's shoulder I knew his career might be over. But there was one way we could make a final bit of money. Something to tide us over at least for a while. So yes, Bobby and I came to New York with a plan of betting money against him. I met with Jiro as soon as we arrived, and that's when he told me about his problems with his family. At the party, I tried to persuade him to do the same as we were doing. At first, he was vehemently opposed to it. He's an honorable man—*was* an honorable man."

A brief expression of grief flashed across her face before she continued.

"I urged him to reconsider, and finally got him to agree to at least come back and talk about it when he wasn't distracted by the party. He had agreed to that much, but he assured me that he didn't intend on disgracing my husband that way. That he was going to find a way to get Miss Walton to give him that money. I assume he had some sort of way of pressuring her into it. Not that he should have had to, it was *his* money."

"But when you got up there he was already dead?"

"I knew it the moment I reached the koi pond."

"Did you handle the body in any way?"

"I went over if only to make sure that it was him. It was so difficult turning him and trying to pull him out, he was so heavy. And when I saw it was him, the way his eyes just stared up at me it was..."

She began crying.

Penelope waited, giving her a moment.

Betty wiped her tears and continued. "He was just staring at me, lifeless. That's when I heard the killer on the other side of the garden, escaping through the stairwell. I got scared and rushed back to the elevators to go back down. Even as the doors closed, I could still see those lifeless eyes staring at me. I'll never forget it."

Bobby reached out to squeeze his wife's hand. "I think my wife has been through enough, Miss Banks. She's told you everything she knows. And now you know my business as well. If that's not enough to help you find out who killed Mr. Ishida, well then I'm sorry, but this is the point at which I think you'd best leave us be."

MURDER IN THE GARDENS

Penelope wanted to ask if she had noticed anything else that might give her more to work with, but her husband had a point. The state Betty was in, she probably wouldn't be all that helpful.

Still, this conversation had been useful, certainly something she'd want to pass on to Detective Prescott. Perhaps Jiro had used some sort of leverage or blackmail to lay on Genevieve Walton in order to get the payment so he wouldn't have to resort to betting against Betty's husband.

All Penelope had to do was find out what that was.

"Thank you for being honest with me," she said as she rose up to leave the suite.

Once again, Penelope took the stairs since it was only one flight back to her floor. While in the stairwell, she recalled what Sam had told her about the soil and water. She studied every nook and cranny of the stairs. If it had continued to the sixteenth floor, that meant whoever had worked with Mandy had been in a suite on this floor. Unfortunately, Pen didn't find a single speck of dirt or water. Whoever had cleaned the stairway had done a thorough job.

"Pineapples," Penelope muttered. Yet another dead end.

When she exited into the hallway of the sixteenth floor she was surprised to see Wendell Dickens there, waiting by her room.

"Ah, Miss Banks, there you are," he said giving her a look that held a mixture of grudging professionalism and firm disapproval. "Your *newest guest* informed me that you were out briefly, but here you are."

"Here I am," Penelope said warily as she approached. "Was there something you needed?"

"Miss Walton would like an audience with you." He arched an eyebrow. "Now."

CHAPTER NINETEEN

Penelope followed Wendell Dickens to the elevator. She couldn't imagine why Genevieve Walton wanted to see her, but she certainly wasn't going to object. It would be the perfect opportunity to interrogate her about whatever was going on with this hotel, particularly the financing.

"Why don't we just take the stairs? It'll be quicker," Penelope said.

Wendell slid his gaze to her, then pursed his lips and nodded. "I suppose."

She followed him up the same set of stairs she had just descended and they exited on the seventeenth floor. Wendell knocked on the door to the Emperor Suite.

"It is open," a woman's voice trilled from inside.

By now Penelope was used to being impressed by the suites of this hotel. The Emperor Suite was no less awe-inspiring than the Presidential Suite had been. As such, she dismissed mentally fawning over the decor, size, and the view of Central Park in favor of the woman sitting down at the small table next to a picture window overlooking the park.

Genevieve Walton was wearing a kimono similar to the one in Penelope's suite. However, hers was decorated with a vibrant floral design. Penelope suspected this was Genevieve's personal kimono. Considering what she had learned about her, it wouldn't have surprised Pen if she owned several.

"Miss Walton, you requested my presence?"

"Please sit, Miss Banks." She gestured to the chair opposite her at the table.

Penelope walked over and sat in the chair.

"That will be all, Wendell." She waved a hand his way without so much as looking at him.

Wendell hesitated, as though he was reluctant to leave. Genevieve simply waited, staring at Penelope with an unreadable expression on her face until he obediently bowed out of the suite, gently closing the door behind him.

Before her on the table were a small ceramic vase and two ceramic cups.

"Join me in a cup of sake."

Penelope wasn't sure if that was a question or demand. It didn't matter as Genevieve poured clearish liquid into both cups. Pen picked up her cup and gingerly took a sip. The liquid was warm and had an odd taste to it. Letitia had said it was warm wine and that is what it reminded Penelope of. It wasn't terrible.

But she wasn't here to drink. She set the cup down after a small sip.

"What is it you wanted to see me about?"

"It has come to my attention that you've been sticking your nose into business that doesn't concern you, Miss

MURDER IN THE GARDENS

Banks." She wagged a finger at her, as though Pen was a young, misbehaving child.

Penelope decided to play dumb. "Whatever do you mean?"

Miss Walton set her cup down and gave Penelope a scathing gaze. "Playing coy with me will do you no favors, Miss Banks. I know you've been looking into Jiro Ishida's death."

"What makes you say that?"

"What did I just say about being coy?"

Penelope studied her, wondering how much of this sake she'd had already. If she was ossified, it might loosen her lips even more. In vino veritas, as the saying went.

"If you want me to be honest and truthful, I expect the same of you."

A subtle smile touched Miss Walton's mouth. "I believe that would work well for both of us."

"Alright, yes I have been looking into Jiro's *murder*. Contrary to what the police recently determined, I don't think it was an accident."

"What makes you say that?"

"I think there are too many people who may have wanted him dead," Penelope said giving her a level gaze.

Miss Walton's brow rose. "If you're looking to me as a suspect, then I'm afraid I'm going to have to disappoint you."

"Why is it you didn't pay him as agreed?"

"Our agreement stipulated an amount, it didn't stipulate a date on which he would receive that amount."

Penelope glared at her. "That's awfully underhanded, don't you think? Most people expect to get paid when the job is done."

"Most people should have made sure that was in the contract when they signed it."

"What possible reason could you have had to withhold his payment? If he had protested too much, I can see how that might have made trouble for you. Quite possibly enough to become a motive for murder."

Genevieve laughed, and Pen now realized she was at least tipsy. "Jiro was in no position to protest too much. He knew exactly why his payment was being withheld."

Penelope sat up straighter, realizing she was learning something new. "And what reason was that?"

Genevieve stared at her for a moment, as though assessing whether or not she was worthy of knowing the truth.

"I suppose now that he's dead, it doesn't matter. His sister had made a promise to a man, Takashi Ando, a promise in which she was intent on reneging."

Penelope couldn't keep from blinking in response. How did Genevieve know about Jiro's sister?

Genevieve's eyes narrowed. "I see that you're familiar with the name. Perhaps you're also familiar with how powerful and wealthy that man is in Japan. How silly it was of Jiro's sister to go back on her promise."

"I suppose I believe in a woman's right to change her mind about the man with whom she plans on spending the rest of her life. I notice you've never been married?"

"I've also never *promised* my hand to a man, only to violate that promise." Miss Walton retorted.

Penelope felt her feathers get ruffled. This was sounding a little too familiar to her own story.

"So this Takashi Ando somehow persuaded you to withhold payment to Mr. Ishida until his sister married him?"

Instead of answering Genevieve picked up her sake and drank, taking a long, hard swallow. She set it down and poured more sake into her cup.

"I'll take that as a yes."

She studied Genevieve, trying to fit this piece into the puzzle that was the murder of Jiro and Mandy.

"Is Takashi Ando the one who's funding this hotel?"

It was brief, but Penelope caught it. The flash of alarm in Genevieve Walton's gaze.

"The funding behind this hotel is none of your concern," she said in a cold, surprisingly lucid voice. "In fact, I do believe you have *overstayed* your welcome here at the Grand Opal Hotel. As the owner, I'm sorry to inform you that we can no longer accommodate you as a guest."

"Are you ousting me from the hotel?" Penelope asked with an incredulous look.

"Yes."

"Because I'm getting too close to the truth?"

"And what truth would that be Miss Banks?"

"Something to do with opium," Penelope chanced asking.

Genevieve stared at her for a moment, then laughed derisively, sloshing the contents of her cup as she did. "How very typical. Anything to do with eastern culture must somehow involve opium. I can see that you aren't quite the sleuth that you think you are, Miss Banks. There is no opium tied to this hotel. Do you think I'm stupid? Every item that came through customs received extra scrutiny as soon as it entered San Francisco, simply because it came from Asia and was tied to a hotel with an eastern theme. This hotel would have failed before it even began. Why on earth would I risk that?"

Penelope was somewhat taken aback by how passionate Genevieve was about this. Most of what she said made sense. It would be stupid to have a hotel that was Asian-themed be involved in the opium trade, especially with recent legislation that seemed to specifically target Asians.

"I take it Mr. Ando back in Japan is an upstanding, legitimate businessman?"

Genevieve returned a sly smile. "Mr. Ando knows how to do what needs to be done. And by that I mean re-opening the doors of communication between Japan and America. Unlike some shortsighted members of Congress, he understands the value of an eastern-western connection, how it can be mutually beneficial. He believed this hotel was just one way of exposing the American public to the modern sophistication and civility that Japan offered. Why do you think no expense was spared in making every aspect of it pure luxury?

"He felt no less enthusiastic about Jiro Ishida himself. He encouraged him and his talents at creating garden masterpieces. All the better to improve the Japanese image in American eyes. More importantly, a man of Japanese heritage who happened to be an American citizen was a *very* valuable asset. Why do you think he was so interested in Jiro's sister? It was strictly business, something she should have seen as a benefit. Now, with Jiro dead, the family is useless to Mr. Ando. I suppose they should be grateful for his death."

"That's a terrible thing to say."

"If you think his death brings me any joy because now I don't have to pay him, you're sorely mistaken. This has been perfectly ruinous for me." She frowned and drank more of her sake.

"Because Jiro is no longer an asset for you either? Is that why you're selling the bonsai trees to Hubert Combs? You're suddenly in need of money? Did Mr. Ando cut you off now that your leverage against Jiro is gone?"

MURDER IN THE GARDENS

Genevieve pulled the cup away and set it back down again, glaring at her. "As I said, Miss Banks, your stay in this hotel is over. I'll have Wendell escort you back down to your hotel room to retrieve your things and go."

So Genevieve did need money, except now Penelope knew the reason why. Genevieve had been used by Takashi Ando, just as much as Jiro and his family had been.

The only problem was that it also took away any motive for murder. Genevieve didn't seem to be involved in any opium business, and she needed Jiro alive for her own purposes.

Penelope rose and walked out without saying goodbye. In the hallway, Wendell still lingered, and Penelope had a sneaking suspicion he had been listening at the door.

"It seems I've been dismissed from the hotel, you'll be happy to know."

She could tell by the look on his face that he did already know, which meant he *had* been listening at the door.

While she had him, she figured it wouldn't hurt to do a little more sleuthing, maybe prove Genevieve wrong about her competency at it. He walked her to the elevator and this time she didn't suggest taking the stairs. The wait would give her time to question him.

"Are you thinking of working for Burnside Development now that the Grand Opal Hotel might be suffering financial difficulties?"

Lucky for Penelope, Wendell would never be the kind of poker player that Gary was. He was incapable of masking his true emotions. His eyes widened in surprise and his face colored with embarrassment.

"H-How do you know about Burnside?"

"So it's true then? You are leaving this hotel?"

His mouth, which had fallen open in surprise, immediately snapped shut, and he studied her through narrowed eyes. "I don't know what you're talking about, Miss Banks."

"Don't you?"

"I am nothing if not loyal to Miss Walton. I've been with her through the entire process of building the Grand Opal Hotel and turning it into the magnificent structure it is. Everything you see in this hotel, every piece of furniture, every person hired, every item on the menu in the restaurants, I have personally overseen. Miss Walton was even generous enough to send me to Japan so that I would have a better understanding of her vision. From the ground floor, up to and including every leaf in that garden, I've had a hand in bringing that vision to fruition. As such, she has been more than generous with me as a reward. I fully plan on staying here with her, by her side through it all. Unlike some people, I know the meaning of loyalty and *discretion*."

Point taken.

Still, Wendell's words didn't matter. Penelope had seen his initial reaction to her question. He wasn't quite as loyal to Miss Walton and the Grand Opal Hotel as he was letting on.

CHAPTER TWENTY

Jane was enjoying tea, still in her kimono when Penelope re-entered the bridal suite.

"It seems that we have been unceremoniously ousted from the Grand Opal Hotel, Jane," Penelope announced as she entered, shutting the door firmly on Wendell.

The sound of it startled Jane and she dropped the cup of tea in her hand causing it to spill all over the coffee table.

"Oh dear! Let me go get towels." Jane popped up from the sofa she was sitting on and ran to the bathroom in her bedroom to get them. She raced back and began using them to blot up the tea.

"Here, let me help," Penelope said, taking the second towel and catching the tea before it dribbled off the table on the other side.

"I'm so clumsy. I guess I'm just not used to so much grandeur."

"Well, enjoy it while it lasts, Jane. I have a feeling we won't be welcome back at the Grand Opal anytime soon. Though..." She wrinkled her nose as she caught the scent of something. She leaned down to sniff the towel and was rewarded with a strong, pungent odor that was almost sickly floral. "Goodness, whatever soap do they wash these towels in?"

She was glad they had used something different for her own towels.

"Yes, I know," Jane said. "See what I meant about the orchids?"

"This is not an orchid smell, Jane. This is—"

She stopped suddenly.

"I've figured it out!"

"What?" Jane asked, staring at her.

"The tree!"

"The tree?"

"Let's pack and go," Pen said, rather than explain. "I want to get to the office and put it all together. Or at least a major part of it."

Jane, bless her heart, had been patient during the drive down to Penelope's private investigation office. Pen had wanted the convenience of the chalkboard Jane had procured for the office in order to organize her thoughts.

When they arrived she instructed Leonard to take her clothes, including the kimonos she had stolen for both her and Jane—she considered it a just compensation for being kicked out. Let the hotel charge her for them later—back to her apartment and drop them there. Then she hurriedly dragged Jane up to their office. Once there they quickly pulled the rolling chalkboard to the center of Penelope's large interior office.

"It was the scent," Penelope said pacing back and forth as she spoke aloud. "Hubert Combs had said something about the azalea plant having an unpleasant odor. Gary said it had a very strong floral smell especially when it was first opened. I thought it was simply the scent of the flowers, but Hubert said that the flowers of that azalea plant don't have a scent."

"So why did it smell?"

"Because someone had doused it with perfume or oil or something to give it a strong scent."

"I'm still not sure what this has to do with the towels," Jane said, a confused look on her face. All she had written on the board was the word "scent" with a question mark.

"Opium."

Jane's face paled.

"Opium?" she whispered in a scandalized voice.

"Opium," Penelope repeated.

Jane looked more confused than ever, but she wrote "opium" on the board, again with a question mark.

"I think the tree was used to ship opium. It was probably hidden underneath the tree in the base of the soil. Hubert mentioned there had been too much soil. Someone had doused it with perfume or oil or something to give it a strong scent. Sam told me last night that there are dogs who can sniff out the scent of opium. So why not cover it up with a strong floral aroma? How many customs agents would know that the flowers of that particular kind of azalea tree don't have a scent? From my experience, most azaleas are rather fragrant. That's probably why the tree was in such poor condition, at least according to Hubert."

Jane dutifully wrote a condensed version of this on the board.

"Then, somehow Mandy found out about it and decided to steal it." Penelope's brow suddenly creased in confusion. "Wait a moment, that doesn't make any sense."

"What doesn't?"

"Why would she steal the whole tree? If the opium was underneath the tree hidden in the soil why not just lift the tree out, take the opium, and then toss the tree away? Why did they hold onto the tree as well?"

"Maybe they liked it, wanted to keep it for themselves? A tiny tree with pink flowers? That sounds lovely," Jane said.

Penelope stopped pacing and stared at her. She thought back to Darlene. Bentley's girlfriend hadn't been the only woman at the party to admire the tree.

"That's a good point, Jane. Why not make it look like a robbery? Everyone would assume the tree had been taken because someone actually wanted the tree itself. Especially if it was to cover up a murder..."

Jane erased what she had written and dutifully wrote, "tree stolen as a cover" on the board underneath "scent" and "opium."

Pen went back to pacing again. "Of course by the time the party starts the odor has somewhat dissipated, but it's still there and strong enough to anyone who gets close. It's also still lingering when it's taken away later on that night and transported right into the Bridal Suite. Specifically, somewhere in the second bedroom of the Bridal Suite, which was supposed to be vacant that night."

"The scent was strongest in the cabinet underneath the vanity where the extra towels were kept," Jane said.

"And there we have it. Unfortunately, the murderer hadn't counted on Penelope Banks and Jane, and I suppose Cousin Cordelia," she said with a grin. "Mandy must have thanked her lucky stars when I requested her for turn down service. That's probably the only reason she brought her cart up, to take away the tree and, more importantly, the opium it was hiding."

"Clever girl..." Jane said in wonder.

"A clever girl who may have killed Jiro Ishida, and inadvertently gotten herself killed as well."

Jane's expression sobered at that reminder.

"But that only gets us back to the idea that there was an accomplice working with her. I can't see her drowning him on her own. I think he caught her and whoever she was working with in the act and there was a physical altercation, during which he hit his head. They must have panicked and decided to make it look like he hit his head and drowned on his own."

"So it was a man?" Jane offered.

"Not necessarily. I think two women could have done it, especially if he was in a daze from his head injury. But let's not focus on male or female let's focus on likely suspects."

Jane got her chalk ready.

Penelope thought back through all the suspects. "It comes back to Bentley, or maybe Darlene. He was the one involved in opium. Everyone else seems to either abhor it or keep a wide berth."

"Perhaps they were all lying?"

It gave Penelope a headache to think about that. Even though she could recall each round of questioning with perfect clarity, she felt exhausted by the idea of analyzing each response, yet again, trying to determine if any of them were telling the truth.

She realized she hadn't had breakfast, and it was already nearing lunchtime.

"I think we should take a much-needed break. I need food in order to fuel my energy. What do you say to lunch?"

Before Jane could respond there was a knock on the

front door of the office. They both stared at each other in surprise, then Jane rushed out to go answer it.

"Detective Prescott!" Jane greeted with delight in her voice.

That was enough to get Penelope walking out to the front office to greet him as well.

"What are you doing here?"

"When I learned you'd been sent packing from the Grand Opal Hotel, I figured you had been meddling," he said with a smile. "As it turns out, that's just what I need."

CHAPTER TWENTY-ONE

Rather than go out to lunch Penelope had Jane get boxed lunches for them to eat in the office. That way they could talk and work at the same time.

While she was gone Penelope couldn't help the smug smile that came to her face as she assessed Detective Prescott.

"So is this you admitting that my womanly wiles may come in handy?"

"That depends on what you discovered while I was working in an *official* capacity."

"Whatever could have brought up this change in you?"

"I tried speaking with Bentley Green. The first words out of his mouth were, 'talk to my attorney.' We're still attempting to get an address for his suitemate."

"Ah, I see how that could be a problem."

"The better question is what did you learn?" His eyes slid to the chalkboard. "Opium?"

Penelope told him everything she had learned, including from Sam Trebant.

"So you know where Mr. Trebant is?"

"*No,* I don't," she said pointedly.

His jaw worked with irritation and she could see him debating whether or not to press the issue. Fortunately, he was smart enough to leave it alone…for now.

"Your conclusions about the tree and the opium make sense. What makes you think any of the people you talked to weren't the accomplice, including Sam?"

"Because Bentley Green has to be the one involved in this. Mandy went straight to his hotel room after collecting the tree from mine. According to Benny, opium is one of his favorite party favors. That means he has at least one connection in this city. Mandy somehow discovered this. She went to his room for a reason. At any rate, we won't know for sure until we talk to him. Or at least until *I* talk to him."

Detective Prescott furrowed his brow in consternation.

"Don't look at me like that. You're the one who said you need some meddlesome person such as myself. In fact, I was told I might be just his type of woman, at least in terms of youth." She looked down at her body, noting that she was lacking at least one thing both Darlene and Mandy had—perhaps a few things.

"I think I could lure him in. He seems to have a preference for shorter dresses." She lifted her own skirt to the same length that Darlene's was at the party. When she saw the way the detective's eyes stared, she lifted them to the much more daring length that Mandy's uniform was. Of course, Pen didn't have the same opaque stockings to protect her modesty.

"I'm not sure what it is you hope to get from Mr. Green, but it certainly doesn't seem like it's information," he said in a wry voice.

"Don't act so scandalized, Detective Prescott," Penelope said enjoying herself, specifically the way he tried so hard to avert his eyes. "Even bathing suits these days go all the way up to Never Never Land. Peter Pan himself would certainly do a little growing up," she added with a laugh.

She heard the front office door open and close behind her.

"Miss Banks!" Jane said in surprise.

Penelope laughed again and let go of her skirts. "I was just introducing Detective Prescott to the future of hemlines. It would seem our Richard is quite the old-fashioned sort. Who knew?"

He arched an eyebrow and gave her a daring look. "I have nothing against modernity, *Penelope*."

She pressed a hand against her chest and feigned a look of shock at the use of her first name.

"What I *do* object to is you endangering yourself unnecessarily. Leaving the topic of opium aside, two people are dead, one of them intentionally, in case you'd forgotten that Miss Clarkson was stabbed to death?"

"Yes, *detective*. Not to worry, my hemlines will stay at an appropriate length. Heaven help me if I have to resort to using my legs in order to get information from people, even men."

"Oh, I don't know, they are quite persuasive. I think they could have worked well for us in the war. Might have ended it sooner if we'd used you as part of our intelligence."

"Detective! To make such tawdry suggestions, and all in front of poor Jane. Look how you've made her blush."

"I'm fine, Miss Banks," Jane said with pursed lips as she set the boxed lunches down on her desk, though her cheeks were a bit pink. "I have tuna, ham, or chicken salad sandwiches."

They gave Jane the first pick and she opted for the tuna salad. Penelope took the chicken salad, and Detective

Prescott took the ham. As they ate, they continued to discuss the case.

"It does seem apparent that Miss Clarkson killed Jiro, most likely without premeditation. Either it was an accident, or she panicked and attacked him, causing him to hit his head. Still, she couldn't possibly—"

"—have done it by herself," Penelope finished for him. "Which means it has to be Bentley Green, then, no? Or maybe Darlene? Maybe all of them were in cahoots!"

"I thought you would have learned by now not to jump to conclusions."

"I'm not jumping to conclusions I'm throwing out possibilities. Surely what I'm saying makes sense?"

"It does, but...thinking about everything you told me, it seems we're forgetting one important thing," Detective Prescott said.

"What's that?" Penelope asked.

"Who is it that had it shipped in the first place? You said it didn't seem like Genevieve Walton was involved. That only leaves a few other people."

Penelope thought on it. "Really just Jiro Ishida and Wendell Dickens, no? Jiro obviously would have been involved in what went into the garden, and Wendell all but said he had a hand in every part of that hotel's construction."

"I'll have to look into this Takashi Ando in Japan. He may very well be involved. The only thing bothering me is...opium doesn't come from Japan. It's mostly India and Turkey. Even here in America, it's a trade that's usually run by the Chinese gangs. They don't tend to play nice with others."

"Maybe that's the perfect cover?" Penelope offered. "Perhaps most customs agents wouldn't look too closely at products from Japan, at least with regard to searching for opium."

"I wouldn't give them that much credit. Anything coming from the Far East is going to be scrutinized. In fact, I'd be willing to bet they all arrive on the same ship. I can't imagine a shipping company traveling all the way to Asia only to stop at Japan and come back. I'll need to make a few phone calls to find out exactly what company handled this shipment, but my guess is Japan is simply a stop on the way back from other ports in Asia."

"So someone gets that opium that comes from another country once the ship docks in Japan. Then they cover it up with the bonsai tree and smuggle it back onto the ship on its way to America."

"Not exactly a simple process. It would take a lot of connections to make it work."

"Unless you were a powerful man in Japan like Takashi Ando." Penelope's eyes brightened as something occurred to her. "Wendell said that Genevieve had sent him to Japan, supposedly to learn more about her vision. What if he decided to make his own business arrangement while he was there? He could easily have it shipped right under her nose. Not difficult to achieve. The woman seems to be perpetually ossified by the looks of it."

"Good detective work," Detective Prescott said with a smile.

"Except," Penelope's brow furrowed. "Why would he be leaving her to go to Burnside Development? To go through all that trouble of setting up this business arrangement only to get a single shipment of opium and then leave?"

"Perhaps he was being blackmailed into doing it?" Jane offered.

"There does seem to be a lot of that going on in this case. Genevieve was holding Jiro's payment back until his sister agreed to marry Takashi. But what would anyone have over Wendell?"

"What if he wasn't leaving to work for Burnside Development, but looking into renting an apartment as a resident?" Detective Prescott said. "According to your father, they cater to the wealthy. What if he expected to come into money on a continual basis? Enough to pay the rent on an apartment owned by Burnside?"

"Good detective work," Penelope said, shooting him a grin.

"So Mr. Dickens was the one who killed Mandy? Because she stole his opium?" Jane asked

"But if that's the case, he wouldn't have been with her when she killed Jiro Ishida, while she was stealing it in the first place," Pen said. "On the other hand, maybe he was working with her all along, though I can't imagine why. Perhaps their partnership went sour and that's why he killed her?"

"Either way, Wendell Dickens is the next person on my list to question." He finished the last bite of his sandwich and stood. "Sorry to leave so abruptly, but I should question him sooner rather than later, now that I have this information. Thank you very much for the sandwiches Miss Pugley, Miss Banks."

"It's Penelope."

"And please call me Jane," Pen's assistant said, almost in a pleading tone.

"Exactly, aren't we all friends?" Penelope said.

"Ladies," he said with a subtle smile. "A good afternoon to you both."

"Perfect! While you do that I'll see what I can get from Bentley Green, and—"

"Absolutely not," the detective said, coming to a stop.

"Why not?"

"You know why not. I'm not putting you in that kind of danger."

"It's not *you* putting me anywhere," Penelope said testily. "What about Darlene, surely I can handle myself with her?"

"No."

Penelope gave him a narrow-eyed look. "I see how it is, you come here use me for information, and then go on your merry way. And to think I told my father you hadn't yet dared to ravish me. Little did I know what a perfect scoundrel you were."

"You told your father about me?" He arched his brow in amusement.

Penelope absently smoothed down her hair feeling slightly embarrassed. "Never mind that. We're still on the subject of you treating me like a child. I bet if I was a man you wouldn't—"

"Yes, I would, if you were a man who had no police training. Do you even own a gun for protection?"

"Not yet," Pen said defensively. The truth was, she could have used one a time or two. Lulu, and for that matter Tommy Callahan, had been urging her to get one. At some point, she probably should. But that was neither here nor there.

"I thought not. Please, Miss Banks, for my own sanity and your own protection allow me to work on this case without having to worry about you?"

"Would you? Worry about me?"

"You make it so easy to do."

Penelope wasn't sure how to interpret that, but she wasn't in the mood to be generous in her thoughts of him right now.

"Fine, *detective*. I wish I could say that it's been a pleasant visit, but, as it is, I feel decidedly violated."

His amusement only seemed to grow. "In which case, I suspect I've earned your father's disapproval."

"You have more in common with him than you think," she snapped.

To her irritation, he laughed.

Penelope felt like a cat that had just had a bucket of water dumped on it.

"I trust this settles it?"

"Yes," she said indifferently, leaning back in her chair arms crossed. "I promise not to talk to Bentley Green."

He narrowed his eyes. "I know better than to trust that."

"What you think is irrelevant to me," she said, her eyes rolling off to the side.

"Since it's quite obvious you intend on ignoring my caution, I'm going to leave you my personal number. I hope that you'll use it to call me before you think of doing anything rash—or, in the more likely scenario, when you find yourself in trouble."

Despite the slight tickle of pleasure she felt running through her, Penelope said, "Why? So you can rob me of information again, then cast me aside?"

Detective Prescott came back, leaning over her desk to write down his phone number. When he was done, he lifted his head to stare at her. He was close enough for Penelope to see every strand of his lush eyelashes.

"I would never cast you aside, Miss Banks." He pulled away leaving her almost breathless. "I'll leave you to your day."

He turned to Jane and tipped his hat. "Miss Pugley."

He left and Penelope waited until she heard the front door of the office closed before she exploded. "Oh, that man!"

"Maybe he has a point, Miss Banks. You have been in danger before on a murder case."

"And came out of it perfectly unscathed, thank you very much. Besides, it isn't as though I plan on walking into an opium den and go around asking questions like a fool. There's a way of going about this that's perfectly safe and still gives me all the information I need. More importantly, what the police need, since they effectively have no way of directly communicating with either Bentley or Darlene."

"You're going to talk to them yourself?"

"Actually, I think right now is the perfect time for a cigarette break."

"But you don't smoke...do you?"

"No, but that doesn't mean I can't light a fire under this case."

CHAPTER TWENTY-TWO

The hardest part of Penelope's mission for the afternoon was access. She needed a way through the Grand Opal Hotel without being seen. Considering Detective Prescott was no doubt already there in the lobby seeking out an interview with Wendell Dickens, that way would have been too risky.

But Pen had always found there was more than one door to getting someplace.

The way New York blocks were set up, the buildings abutted each other, all of them facing outward. It was rare to find an open alleyway, usually one had to go through the buildings.

Thus, as it turned out, Penelope did in fact have to use her legs.

She wandered around the block on which the Grand Opal Hotel was situated until she found a gate that led to a small narrow path to the back part of the building. It was of course blocked by a locked gate. But that was no barrier for Penelope. She had recently perfected the art of getting past such an obstacle.

She reached up and pulled a bobby pin from her hair and went to work on the lock until she managed to open it. Once she eased through, quietly closing the gate behind her, she trekked down the path until she was in the alleyway.

As soon as she reached it, she was reminded why these areas were so closed off. This was usually where each building kept its garbage. The smell hit her as soon as she reached the alley.

She wound her way past cans and rodents and, worst of all, terrible stenches. By the time she got to the back door of the Grand Opal, she could understand why the staff preferred to go to the gardens on the roof to smoke their cigarettes.

She waited as far as possible from the garbage while still being able to view the door. She had timed it just right, such that—

Sure enough, the door opened and Rosie popped out still in her day clothes.

"Hiya, Rosie."

The maid nearly jumped out of her skin, and Penelope felt bad for surprising her.

"Miss Banks, you nearly scared me half to death!"

"I'm sorry, I didn't mean to frighten you. I should have realized you'd still be shaken from what happened with Mandy."

She flashed a brief smile. "Yeah, I don't think I can ever go back up on the roof again. Still, I have to pay the rent, so here I am." She pulled out her cigarette. "Except now I don't know if I'll even be able to do that."

"Why not?"

"Mr. Dickens just told us we're getting a pay cut. I guess

all this murder has been bad for business." She lit her cigarette and took a puff.

"I think it might be a bit more than that. You might want to warn your fellow employees that more pay cuts might be coming down the line. They might as well get a head start on looking for new employment."

Rosie stared at her. "You don't say?"

"The financing is a bit shaky is what I *will* say." She tilted her head to consider Rosie. "If you happen to need temporary employment in between finding something new, and don't mind working at a private residence, I'm looking for a new maid for my apartment."

"Really?"

"Really. If it works out, it can become a permanent situation."

"That's swell, Miss Banks. I've never worked for a private home before." She wrinkled her brow in confusion. "Is that why you're here?"

"No, actually I was hoping I could bribe you into getting a bit of information for me."

She pulled out the standard five-dollar bill and Rosie's eyes understandably grew wider. Then they narrowed with wariness. "What is it you want?"

"I just need you to look at the register from the front desk to see if you could get Darlene's information? She was the woman staying with Bentley Green. At the very least I need a last name. If you can get either a phone number or address it would be the berries."

Rosie's eyes landed on the five-dollar bill with greed in them, then she grinned. "I think I can do that. It's so easy to tease Mr. Dickens. I know he only hired me 'cause he likes the way I look, even in these frumpy maid's uniforms. It's the same for Leticia and..." her face suddenly fell and she put away her cigarette. "...at least it *was* for Mandy."

"This information might help me find out who killed her," Penelope said gently, bringing Rosie's attention back to her.

"Anything you need Miss Banks. I'll get right on it."

"Thank you," Penelope said handing over the money.

When Rosie went back inside Penelope moved further down to get away from the garbage. Staring at the containers, something occurred to her.

"Ugh," she sighed, as she realized what she needed to do. She walked over to pull the lids away. It was while riffling through the third can that she found it.

The azalea tree.

It was buried underneath a pile of unpleasantness. Even then, the smell of the tree, now rapidly rotting, overwhelmed the senses. This lent credence to the idea that the tree was nothing more than a cover for the opium, or whatever it had been hiding. Mandy had probably dumped it here after the police had finished searching for it.

Pen would obviously tell Detective Prescott about this... as soon as she had a bath.

Rosie returned and the look on her face indicated she had discovered something.

"All I could get from the register was her name, Darlene Fairbanks. However, one of the bellboys, Jimmy, saw me looking and he told me that he'd overheard her saying something about working in the hosiery department at Gimbel's."

"That's more than I could have hoped for, Rosie," Penelope said, pleased. "Again, if you're interested in changing jobs, you come by my apartment, say nine a.m. this Friday? That should be before your shift starts here, right?"

Penelope thought surely the case would be solved by then.

"Gee, thanks again, Miss Banks," Rosie said after Penelope gave her the address.

"You're welcome, I'll see you then."

Penelope left the same way she had come, by going through the gate whose lock she had originally picked. Unfortunately, she could smell herself even more once she was back on the sidewalk. Blessedly her apartment was only a few blocks up so she walked the distance, ignoring the looks of disgust from the people she passed.

Chives greeted her at the door and was tactful enough not to show any hint he could smell the *eau de garbage* wafting from her.

"Good news, Chives," she greeted. "We may have a temporary solution to our maid problem. I have one coming to interview on Friday."

"Very good, Miss Banks," he said, professional as ever, but she could sense the note of relief in his voice.

She had to pass by the living room to get to her own bedroom and found Cousin Cordelia with the white Persian cat they had adopted, Lady Dinah, in her lap. She kept her distance so as not to offend her cousin's nose.

"Why Penelope, I was beginning to think you'd been murdered in that hotel. It's been so long since I've seen you."

"I hadn't realized one night was so long," Pen teased. "Did Lady Di miss me as well? Speaking of which where are—"

Penn was unable to get the sentence out before three kittens, who were steadily growing into cats, came bounding into the living room. The one that was perfectly orange headed straight for her stockinged legs as per usual. Blessedly, the scent of her kept him away and he reeled back, his little body nearly tumbling.

"Serves you right for constantly going to war with my stockings. I should take it out of your food allowance."

He mewled softly and decided his sister's tail was an acceptable foe instead.

"Gracious, what is that odor, Penelope?"

"Something I plan on remedying right now, cousin," Penelope said, rushing off to her bedroom.

She ran a bath, using a generous amount of lavender oil. Hopefully, it would be enough to rid herself of the odor.

After all, she had a trip to Gimbel's department store to make.

CHAPTER TWENTY-THREE

Penelope had not only had to bathe to smell acceptable but wash her hair as well. By the time she was fully dry, clothed, and somewhat presentable, it was near evening.

She arrived at Gimbel's and headed straight for the hosiery department. Once there, she searched for the familiar brown bob among the women surrounding her. After several minutes with no luck, she finally approached a woman behind the counter.

"How can I help you?" she greeted, giving Pen a broad, professional smile.

"I was looking for a young woman who I was told works here, Darlene Fairbanks?"

The young woman's eyes lit up. "Darlene? She and I share an apartment. How about that?" Then, her eyes quickly narrowed. "What did you want with her?"

Penelope remembered the conversation she'd overheard Darlene having with Bentley at the party.

"I represent a Mr. Marshall," Penelope said making up a name on the spot. "He's starting production on a new play and he is very interested in giving Miss Fairbanks a very specific role."

"Is that so?" The woman's face fell so much, Penelope almost felt bad about the subterfuge. Apparently Darlene wasn't the only hopeful for the stage.

"It's a small part really, tiny even, but he is very eager to speak with her. Do you know where I might find her?"

"She didn't bother coming in to work today, did she?" The woman sniffed. "I think that says a lot about her reliability, don't you?"

"Was she home sick? Perhaps I could call or stop by your apartment?"

The woman pouted. "I don't see what's so special about Darlene. I'm a much better actress, just so's you know. Maybe I can audition for this Mr. Marshall. The name is Sally, Sally Follet. I'm thinking of changing it to Sally Sinclaire though. I think that sounds more glamorous, don't you?"

"I see nothing wrong with Sally Follett, it's a perfectly fine name. But regarding Miss Fairbanks, perhaps I could get her address or phone number?" She quickly added. "Of course, I would make sure to put in a good word for you with Mr. Marshall."

Hopefully that would get her talking.

"Actually I'm just about to get off work in five minutes. I can take you straight there myself, perhaps we can talk about this play along the way?"

That was the last thing Penelope wanted. She hadn't planned on maintaining an entire conversation in order to get information about Darlene.

"Actually I'm rather in a hurry—"

"Oh, that's no bother, just give me one moment." Sally walked over to another woman further down the counter and briefly said something to her. The woman looked at her, then looked past her at Penelope, then back again, and then nodded.

Sally came back to Penelope with a smile. "Annie has agreed to cover these last five minutes for me. Let me just get my things and we can go!"

Penelope wasn't sure what to say to that. If she backed out now, she'd never get to talk to Darlene.

"I usually take the subway," Sally said as they walked out. She gave Penelope a pointed look. "That isn't a problem is it?"

"Why don't we take a taxi instead? My treat."

This was obviously what Sally was hoping for and she readily agreed. At least it would be quicker than the subway. Then again, there was traffic, and as it turned out, Sally and Darlene lived on 8th Street. Fortunately, Sally was the talkative type, intent on showing off her many talents and attributes that were "far superior to Darlene's."

"Here we are. The third building up," she instructed the driver who came to a stop in front of it. Penelope paid him, then followed Sally out of the car and up the steps to the front door.

Sally stopped just as she stuck the key in the lock to the front entrance. "So what do you think? You think maybe this Mr. Marshall will consider me instead of Darlene?"

"I'm afraid Mr. Marshall is looking for a specific type. However, as I said, I will absolutely be certain to pass along your name." That did nothing to get Sally to turn the key. Penelope could see that she was going to be difficult. "Actually, from everything I saw in the taxi, I'm inclined to suggest using you instead of Darlene. Of course, I'd have to speak with Darlene first, it's only fair."

That was enough to appease Sally, and she continued to

open the door. She blathered the entire walk up two flights of stairs. By the time they reached the third floor, Penelope wondered if this was worth it. Sally had the kind of high-pitched voice that may have worked well greeting women in a department store but it was grating on the ears after too long.

"Home sweet home!" Sally actually sang in a falsetto as she opened the door. It made Penelope wince.

Pen looked around at the apartment, which was neat and clean but the sort of basic, utilitarian apartment one would expect two young women working in a department store in Manhattan to have. She stood near the doorway waiting for Darlene to make an appearance. After a moment, she turned to Sally with a questioning look.

"Is she not home?"

Sally shrugged. "I don't really keep up with her. Maybe she's with that fella of hers."

"Fella?"

"Again, I don't keep up. But I do know he's much older and he has *no* intention of marrying her," she added with a smirk.

"Oh, well..."

Sally seemed to be sensing that she was about to lose her one shot at fame. She came in closer to Penelope with an ingratiating smile. "Say, that's a really nice perfume you got on, what's it called? Where did you get it?"

"It's just lavender oil I put in my bath."

"It smells real nice, like a field of flowers," Sally said, her eyes piercing Penelope. "Why don't you stay and have some coffee. I'm sure Darlene won't be long."

Without waiting for a response, she went over to the small kitchenette and filled a pot with water, then put it on the stove.

MURDER IN THE GARDENS

"You like sugar, milk?"

Penelope realized she might as well stay long enough for coffee now that Sally had started, which was probably her plan all along. "Sugar is fine thank you."

Sally smiled and grabbed the sugar bowl to place at the small kitchen table, thus inviting Penelope to sit down.

Penelope went over and sat down on the chair which was right next to a tiny window that faced nothing but a brick wall. With that sad view, she instead allowed her eyes to roam over the visible areas of the apartment. They landed on the wastebasket in the corner of the kitchen.

All this talk of her lavender oil made her think. She had found the azalea tree in the garbage behind the Grand Opal Hotel. She wondered what evidence she might find here in this bit of trash.

Penelope reached into her purse in search of something to throw away. Her hand latched onto the piece of paper Detective Prescott had used to write down his phone number. Fortunately, Penelope had already glanced at it so she knew the number was etched into her memory forever. With a smile, she stood up and walked over to the trash. At Sally's questioning look she just held up the crumpled piece of paper.

"You don't mind if I throw this away do you?"

Sally presented her with a Gimbel's smile. "Of course not!"

Penelope tossed the piece of paper in and lingered. The can was full, but the top layer didn't reveal much, mostly papers, ripped stockings, and coffee grounds.

"Oh drat!" Pen said, as though she hadn't meant to throw it away. She reached in and pushed aside the trash on top to dig around. She eventually saw the edge of a brown box. She pushed aside everything covering it, cringing all

221

the while. Sure enough, "Gregory's" stared right back at her.

She stood back up and turned around to find Sally giving her a look that reflected just how oddly she was behaving.

"I see the box for Gregory's. Darlene must have really liked those donuts."

Sally's brow creased with even more bewilderment, then smoothed out as she shrugged and returned to making the coffee. "Yeah, not that she saved any for me. That fella of hers may like the way she looks now, but she keeps eating like that and she's gonna turn into a real porker. Then who'll have her? Those Broadway producers don't like girls to be too big these days. I, for one, don't even eat breakfast. Just black coffee, thank you very much. Still, she coulda at least offered, ya know?"

"So you never even saw them?"

"Not a one. She must a stuffed 'em down her gullet before coming back home," Sally said with a snide laugh.

With this new and very illuminating clue, Penelope was less inclined to entertain Sally's company.

"Do you have a phone I can use?" she asked hopefully.

"There's one on the first floor for everyone in the building to use," Sally said, turning to her with a frown.

"Thank you," Penelope said rushing out.

"Hey wait a minute, what about talking to Mr. Marshall about me?" She heard Sally call out after her.

"I'll talk to him!" Penelope lied as she rushed down the stairs. She found the phone behind the stairs and picked up the receiver to connect to the number Detective Prescott had given her. After a while, the operator got back on and insisted that there was no one on the other line.

MURDER IN THE GARDENS

"Pineapples!" He must have been still questioning Wendell Dickens.

"I'm sorry?" the operator asked.

She instead gave the operator the number for the 10A precinct, just in case. After connecting, Penelope asked to speak to Detective Prescott only to be told he wasn't in.

"Pineapples," Pen repeated after hanging up, even more frustrated. She stared at the phone, nibbling her bottom lip in thought as to what to do next.

"Well, it seems you've found me."

Penelope spun around to find Darlene walking through the front door, glaring at her.

CHAPTER TWENTY-FOUR

"Miss Fairbanks," Penelope said finally catching her breath after being surprised by the sudden appearance of Darlene.

Darlene arched an eyebrow. "Well, it seems you know a lot more about me than I know about you. Perhaps you can start with *your* name?"

"Penelope Banks."

"No detective with you today?" At Pen's surprised look, Darlene coughed out a sardonic laugh. "He had it written all over him when I saw you two together."

"I'm here alone...unofficially."

"You have a lot of people wondering where you've been today."

"Why do you think I was gone? So much for that, I guess."

"I'm just here to talk."

"Spare me the banana oil. What is it you really want?"

Pen considered her. She could tell Darlene was a lot savvier than she had put on back at the party. "I'm trying to find out if you killed Mandy, and perhaps Jiro."

Darlene stared at her for a moment, then she broke out in laughter. "Oh honey, that's good."

"Laughter is sometimes a reaction to panic I've found. Did I uncover something you didn't want me to by coming here?"

"I dunno, did you?" Darlene said, an eyebrow arched.

"I saw the box of donuts in your trash upstairs. But they weren't really holding donuts, were they? At least not by the time you left the Grand Opal Hotel. Is that how you stole the opium right from underneath the nose of Bentley and Mandy?"

Darlene studied her once again, a slow smile spreading her lips. "You ain't as dumb as you look."

Penelope steeled her gaze. "Smart enough to have you figured out."

"You think so?"

"Yes, and I'm sure the detective I was with will be more than interested in what I've found."

Darlene laughed again and shrugged. "Go on then, call him. I'd love to see the look on his face when it ain't what he expects—opium, I mean."

Penelope considered herself a good judge of when someone was bluffing, at least in the moment. She had to admit that murder cases had put that talent to the test. It was one thing to figure out someone's tell in poker, quite another to determine if someone was lying to save themselves from the electric chair.

But she was quickly learning.

And Darlene was definitely covering something up.

"You're lying."

Darlene studied her for a moment, then exhaled. "Oh, what the hell, you got me."

Penelope blinked in surprise. She hadn't expected that.

"But it ain't what you think."

"Then what is it?"

"You got any kale on you?"

Penelope narrowed her eyes. "Yes, why?"

"Because you's buying me a drink."

"Is that so?"

"*Yeah*, that's so. There's a place just at the end of the block." Without waiting for a response, she turned on her heels and walked right back out the front door.

Penelope stared after her, mouth parted at the absolute gall of the woman. Still, this was one gift horse she wasn't about to look in the mouth. She followed Darlene out.

It did occur to her that this might be some kind of trap, but when they entered the street there were enough people walking around to set her mind at ease. That subsided when they reached a green door. It was a well-known symbol for a speakeasy. But Penelope had learned looks could be deceiving.

Darlene's expression was unreadable as she knocked three times, then once, then twice. It took a moment but the door was eventually opened just a sliver.

Rather than utter a password Darlene dug into her purse and offered a small card. Penelope recognized it as a membership card many speakeasies used as the only means of ingress.

"Well, you're certainly in like sin aren't you?" Penelope observed with a wry smile. Darlene just offered one in return as the door was opened for them.

The space was large and had obviously once been a legitimate bar. It was now quite packed. Pen wondered if it was doing even more business under Prohibition than it had before. There was a certain thrill people got from what many saw as a harmless crime. Darlene led her in and they found space at the bar to order drinks.

Darlene leaned in and smiled at the man tending bar. "Hiya Danny, I'll have gin, straight up as usual."

That happened to be Pen's own choice of poison and if a card-carrying member trusted this place not to serve bathtub rot, she was willing to trust it. "I'll have the same."

When they were served—Penelope paying as expected—she turned to Darlene with a piercing look. "Okay, start talking."

Darlene led them to a more private corner and leaned against the wall to take a long sip and swallow. "What do you want to know?"

"You know what I want to know," Pen said, exasperated. "Did you kill Jiro? Mandy? Did you steal the opium?"

"No, no, and no," Darlene said and nonchalantly sipped her drink.

Penelope gripped her glass and felt like throwing it right in her face. This case was becoming perfectly exasperating. Perhaps that would snap Darlene out of this insouciance.

Instead, she took a breath before continuing. "Tell me what happened when Mandy entered your suite."

Darlene sipped again, studying Pen over the glass. Then, she pulled it away and swallowed.

"I knew what was on that girl's mind from the moment she approached Benty at the party. Whisperin' in his ear, all when I was right there?" She gave Pen an appalled look. "Anyway, Benty thought I was sleepin' off the gin he'd plied me with later on that night."

"So you were awake for it all?"

"Darn right I was. A girl's gotta protect what's hers, and that Mandy wasn't shy, if you get my drift. But aside from all the flirting, she had something else he wanted, it seemed.

That's when I *really* got curious. I went to go listen at the bedroom door."

"What did you hear?" Pen said, feeling her heart beat faster.

"Opium. Bentley said, 'if it is what you say it is then it should be worth quite a bit.'" Darlene revealed the amount, and Penelope nearly choked on the sip she had just taken.

"No!"

"Yes," Darlene said with a devilish grin.

"Certainly an amount worth killing for?" Pen suggested.

Darlene's eyes narrowed. "Which I didn't do. Didn't have to."

"How is it you stole it then?"

"After all that drinkin' with Miss Mandy, he was out like a light. I knew he liked to sleep in. That's when I got the donuts."

Pen waited for an explanation.

Darlene laughed. "It was actually pretty smart, if I do say so myself. Miss Mandy had gotten her claws into Bentley. He even gave her one of my dresses, can you believe that? Yeah, I hated the thing—everyone knows purple in *any* shade ain't my color, especially floral numbers—but still, it's the principle of the thing! I figured I deserved a parting gift, so I took mine. Laid those donuts out on a plate and put the package Mandy had brought in the box, then put it in the trash like I had tossed it. That at least helped hide the smell. When we checked out, we went our separate ways. But I circled back, claiming I'd forgotten something and that's when I got the box.

"You shoulda seen his face when he woke up and the package was gone. Naturally, he suspected me, but all I had to do was play dumb. After all, I'd been fast asleep during his little tryst, hadn't I?" Darlene said in a girlish voice that reflected the version of her Pen had seen at the party with Bentley. "He probably thought I was too stupid to plan such a thing. Staying there with him instead of running off after I stole it was the smart part of it. If I really had taken it, why would I stick around? I was the one to suggest maybe some maid had come in and stolen it. That one had him raging. If you're looking for someone to point the finger at as to who killed Mandy, my money would be on him."

"So you *did* steal the opium."

"No," Darlene said, back to idly sipping her gin with an impish smile.

"I'm this close to calling the police down right now, maybe close up your favorite gin mill while I'm at it, sweetheart."

Darlene just heaved a heavy sigh and rolled her eyes. "It wasn't opium, you dumb Dora."

Pen ignored the insult in light of this news. "What? But you said—"

"I said I heard the word 'opium.' Mandy was another dumb Dora who didn't even realize what she had. It was wrapped in all this cheesecloth and wax paper and when I opened it...." She wrinkled her nose in disgust. "It was a big pile of dried tea leaves, except I ain't never smelled tea like that. It was awful."

"What did it smell like?"

"Like—to be honest, it smelled like someone had relieved themselves on it. How disgusting is that?"

"What?" Pen said in surprise.

"I'm not sure what opium smells or looks like, but I do know tea leaves. My auntie used to read 'em for fun."

Pen was still thinking about this revelation, and something still didn't fit.

MURDER IN THE GARDENS

"Surely Bentley would have known right away it wasn't opium?"

Darlene shrugged and sipped her drink. "I don't think he even opened the package. It didn't seem like it when I got my hands on it."

"How do I know you aren't just making this up? This story doesn't really make any sense."

"Check the garbage in my apartment building. It's right there."

"I did, and I certainly didn't smell what you're suggesting."

"Not that one, the main trash for the whole building out back. You'll smell it then. I mean, once you get past the wrapping I redid. I wasn't about to leave it in my apartment."

"I will," Pen said, studying her for tells.

Darlene just smiled, gave her an even look, and sipped her drink. She wasn't bluffing.

"Why was Bentley so mad the next morning then? Surely he wouldn't have been that mad over tea leaves? Were they some kind of special tea? Perhaps mixed with some kind of opiate substance? Maybe that's why it was worth so much?"

"Trust me, I looked through that stuff more closely than a kid huntin' for Easter eggs. It was nothing but tea, just with a weird smell. Had to leave the window open all day just to get the smell out of my bedroom."

Pen thought back to the night of Jiro's murder. "What was Bentley doing in the lobby that night?"

"What?"

"When Gary was found with the body, and the police were called, Bentley was held in the lobby with everyone else who hadn't been in their room at the time. Why wasn't he in the suite with you?"

"Probably went for more of his cigarettes. He was running low, being that he never stops smoking the things. At least when he ain't doing something else with his mouth." She rolled her eyes and grimaced.

"At that time of night, he went out for cigarettes?"

Darlene coughed out a laugh. "You'd be surprised what the rich can get when they want. There are places that cater to every need, at any time of night."

Pen wasn't so sure. And this once again made Bentley a prime suspect in both murders. Except...if he'd been on the roof with Mandy, why would he not have just taken the package then? Why hide it in the Bridal Suite when the Honeymoon Suite was right there?

No, it had to be someone else who helped Mandy kill Jiro and steal the package.

"As far as you know, *is* Bentley involved with using opium?" Perhaps Benny had been mistaken about that aspect of it?

"Oh, absolutely. Those parties of his? He tries to keep it hush-hush, and only certain people know. He was real upset about that golfer from out of town knowing. Wondered how some 'inbred hick'—his words not mine—had learned about his little habit. He only likes to associate with other rich fellas like himself. I've never tried the stuff, of course. I know to keep my wits about me, especially with him."

Which means Bentley would know it if he saw it. None of this was making any sense.

"Could he have opened it and just repackaged it well?" Pen asked.

"It didn't look like it, and I would have smelled it in the

hotel room if he had. Then again with those clove cigarettes of his, who would have known? Sally always says I come back to the apartment smelling like Christmas. Then, of course, there was that tree Mandy brought in. That was certainly a smell that lingered, even after she took it away."

And then put it in the hotel trash.

"Okay, drink up, Darlene. You're taking me to this trash can in your apartment building."

Darlene met her with an incredulous look, her eyes scanning the nice dress she had on. "I hope you know a decent cleaner."

CHAPTER TWENTY-FIVE

Thirty minutes later, Penelope was once again in need of a bath. She was using the phone in Darlene's apartment building to call Detective Prescott. She had in fact found the package Darlene claimed was tea. And yes, it did in fact smell like someone had relieved themselves on it.

"Detective," Pen said, pleased at having finally gotten through to him. "I found out what the tree was disguising."

"You did?" She could hear the censuring tone in his voice, but he was still curious.

"You have to come here to see it. I can't really understand it."

She gave him the address and hung up. It was that hour of the evening when those with jobs were returning home. A man entered the apartment building and had to pass by her to get to the stairs. The flirtatious smile he had on his lips when he first saw her quickly transitioned to a curl of revulsion as he smelled her upon passing.

"Zounds," Pen muttered to herself. The things she'd had to rifle through to get to Darlene's package were as unpleasant as that behind the Grand Opal Hotel.

When Detective Prescott finally arrived, she put up a hand. "Don't say anything about the way I smell. I had to do a lot of the dirty work for this case."

"A woman who is willing to get a bit dirty for the sake of justice is something to be admired, not scorned," he said with a grin as he approached. He came to an instant stop once he got close enough to smell her. "Oh—yes, that's bad."

"What did I just say?" she accused. "At any rate, it's your turn. I left the package in the trash so as not to taint the evidence. Heaven knows I had to dig through enough garbage just to uncover it. You're welcome for that."

"Thank you in advance?"

She laughed. "Don't thank me yet."

Penelope led him to the back and showed him the trash, explaining everything she'd learned that day—including discovering the azalea tree. He stopped to call his precinct to recover it from behind the hotel. Then, he followed her to the back alley.

Pen had told him to bring a flashlight, being that the sun was setting. He used it to light the inside of the can where the package was mostly uncovered. He reached into his pocket and pulled out a handkerchief.

The package was a decent size, but Penelope admired the way his large hand was able to take hold of it and pull it out without leaving his fingerprints on it. It was haphazardly wrapped and he set it down on the lid of another can. He used the handkerchief to pull it open to reveal a large pile of...tea leaves.

He leaned in to sniff and instantly pulled back. "Well, she was right about that part. And looking at it, yes it is just tea leaves."

"See what I meant about it not making sense?"

"Not entirely," he said in thought. "Opium tends to have a slight ammonia smell associated with it."

That was something new for Penelope. She hadn't thought about what opium actually smelled like.

"I did check on the shipping company used, and as I thought, they hit several ports of call around Asia with Japan being the final stop before coming to America."

"So the tea was used to transport opium?"

He stroked his chin as he studied the contents. "It wouldn't have left this much of a lingering scent, I don't think. Plus, this is a lot of tea. I'm thinking about the size of the pot that plant was most likely in. When you factor in the roots of the tree and the large amount of soil, and this much tea, that doesn't leave room for a lot of opium. Certainly not an amount to go to this much trouble for."

"So we're back to it not making sense again?" Penelope asked.

"No, it has to make sense. Let's just think."

"Can we at least think someplace I can take a quick bath or at least change? Come to my apartment; you can join Cousin Cordelia and me for dinner."

His eyes rolled over to meet hers, inscrutable for a moment. Then he grinned. "I thought I was the one who was supposed to be asking you to dinner at some point."

"Since you seem to be taking your time with that, I might as well be forward. Modern times call for modern solutions," she replied with a coy smile.

"I have a better idea. I'll meet you at your apartment and we can discuss the case. As for dinner, I'd rather our first time not be this...tainted." He sniffed as though to make the case. "Also, I have certain affairs to get in order before I become quite that familiar with you, Penelope."

Suddenly Pen didn't care how horrible she smelled.

Was he finally making a move? In such an odd way? And what did he mean by getting his affairs in order?

"I think it's obvious by now that I am quite fond of you, and you've certainly never been shy about your feelings," he said with a softer smile. "But when I do finally ask you out to dinner, I'd like to make sure everything is done properly. And hopefully I can officially ask you someplace a bit more romantic than next to garbage cans in an alley."

Penelope laughed, her heart beating wildly. It was frustrating, confounding, and thrilling all at once—just like the man himself was.

"I suppose I'll see you in an hour then."

An hour later, Pen was freshly bathed, smelling like lavender once again. She stood in her closet wondering what to wear. Her eyes fell on the kimono she had stolen and she flirted with the idea of wearing that to greet Richard. The name sounded wonderfully foreign in her head, she was so used to calling him Detective Prescott.

He had all but confirmed they were something more than simply occasional work partners.

Pen decided on a light blue gauzy dress with a paisley print and black velvet bow on one shoulder. After dressing, she joined Cousin Cordelia waiting in the living room.

Chives announced his arrival not a moment later.

"Good evening, Miss Banks," he greeted, using her formal address after noting her cousin was there.

"Shouldn't we hide, er, certain substances, Penelope?" Cousin Cordelia said in a panic.

"Richard doesn't care about our bootleg alcohol."

"I'm willing to turn a blind eye to it tonight, Mrs. Davies."

"We'll go into the library. I wouldn't want to upset you with talk about the murder, Cousin."

"Yes, dear," Cousin Cordelia said wearily. "I've had enough of that the past few days."

They escaped to the library and sat down on the couch in the middle of the room.

"Lavender?" He asked, now that he was close enough to smell her.

"And a lot of it," she said with a laugh. "I certainly needed it."

"A vast improvement," he said with a grin.

"Same for yourself," she mused. "It's funny, this whole case started in a garden, and thus far we've only been introduced to the most horrid scents. It's rather—"

She stopped short.

"What is it?"

"The cloves!"

"What about cloves?" Richard said, studying her.

"Darlene said she usually left Bentley smelling like Christmas. You know what else smells like Christmas? Pumpkin pie! Rosie said her dress smelled like pumpkin-pie flavored gin. It was Bentley's cigarettes, they smell like cloves, which is one of the main ingredients in pumpkin pie. He had also plied Darlene with gin, so he had some in his suite. He must have spilled some on Mandy's uniform—or rather Rosie's uniform!"

"So Mandy was in Rosie's uniform that night?"

"I thought hers was just short and tight in order to entice him, but no. She was wearing Rosie's uniform. No doubt because hers was wet and soiled, and probably covered in blood from Jiro's wound. I'm thinking Bentley gave her one of Darlene's dresses to change into. Mandy didn't even bother to clean her uniform before hanging it back up."

"Well, we figured Mandy was involved with Jiro's murder so that makes sense," Detective Prescott said.

"Yes..." Penelope said. Something was still nagging at her about this but she couldn't place it. It would eventually come to her. Right now, she wanted to help unravel this business about the tea leaves.

"At any rate, I think I finally have the tea figured out," Richard continued.

"Really?" Pen said.

"This may have been a test shipment. Use something with a similar scent to opium, cover it with the smell of the tree, and see if it passes through customs without problems."

Penelope frowned. "That doesn't explain why Bentley was upset, unless—"

"He was involved in the smuggling," he finished for her. "It could be why he may not have even bothered opening the package Mandy brought. He already knew what it was. Obviously, she *didn't* know what it was."

"But how? He had no involvement with the Grand Opal Hotel, specifically the shipments? If anything he was a rival. They certainly wouldn't have allowed him that much control and access to what they had shipped. In fact, I'm certain he was the one Betty claimed had offered Jiro the job for future gardens. At the very least he would need an inside accomplice. Someone involved with the shipment." Pen scrutinized Richard. "Speaking of which, how did your interrogation of Wendell Holmes go?"

"He tried stonewalling me with the insistence on an attorney. But the moment I mentioned dragging the hotel into it, including Miss Walton, he couldn't talk fast enough.

MURDER IN THE GARDENS

The apartment? She had promised it to him, including the salary to afford it. His reward for loyalty. He even showed me the letter of intent Miss Walton had provided to guarantee his income. That appears to be on hold now that Mr. Ando back in Japan is withholding funding. He did seem awfully disappointed at the idea that his hopes for new and improved luxury accommodations were dashed."

"I still think it's him. Who else could it be? Jiro had no reason to get involved in such a thing before Genevieve withheld his payment at the last moment."

"Just in case, let's take a closer look at all the suspects again."

Penelope nodded. "Bobby Paxton had an injured shoulder, so it would have been difficult for him to help Mandy move Jiro to the pond and drown him. Unless he's faking it?"

"Working all the way from Georgia would have been difficult. Besides, he regularly wins purses that amount to tens of thousands, even hundreds of thousands on occasion. I doubt he'd throw that away for the sake of getting involved in opium," Richard said.

"You follow golf?"

"I've been known to play a round or two," he said, offhandedly. "However, he did know about Bentley's connections with opium."

"Which Bentley was upset about, indicating they weren't in cahoots," Pen pointed out.

"Then there's Betty, his wife."

"If she killed Jiro it would have been an accident. I believe she genuinely liked and admired him."

"I don't believe her to be involved. She had no reason to alert anyone to his body, thus getting herself involved. We never would have known she was on the roof otherwise."

Richards's eyes pierced Penelope. "Which gets us to Sam, who she heard escaping at the same time she did."

"But why would he kill Jiro?"

"Mandy had been the one to ask him about opium. Maybe he was her accomplice despite denying it?"

"But why even tell me about that at all?"

"Maybe she double crossed him and he wanted to point the finger squarely at her?"

"Only for anyone with any sense to realize she couldn't have drowned Jiro on her own, and then point the finger right back at him as an accomplice? I've played cards with the man. He's far too cunning for that. He would have more likely misdirected me."

"Okay, let's move on to Hubert Combs."

"He already has money," Pen pointed out.

"One thing I've learned about the wealthy is that they are often keen for more."

"Oh, I don't know about that. *I'm* quite satisfied with my lot. Five million is more than enough to sustain me, I think," she teased.

"Just one of the many admirable qualities about you, Penelope," Richard said with a wry grin.

Penelope smirked and rolled her eyes. "Getting back to Mr. Combs."

"Right, well, he was an advisor in the development of the hotel. Perhaps that translated to being involved with the shipping? He mentioned he'd been to Asia quite often. He'd certainly have the connections to get an opium trade going. But we searched his suite and, just as with the others, the letter opener was still there, good as new."

Penelope pondered that. Something about connections...

She stood up and paced to help herself think. She revisited everything she'd learned, replaying every conversation in her head.

"What if...he had access to more letter openers?"

"You mean based on his connection to the hotel? It's something we can easily ask about. But it would be stupid of him to ask for a replacement after he'd used his to kill Mandy. And to specifically have one or more ahead of time would be odd."

"Unless he had access to an entire lot of them!" Pen announced, the answer finally hitting her.

"How do you mean?"

"Gary mentioned selling a lot of the, er, *surplus* products he acquired while he was working construction on the hotel before it opened." Richard's brow rose as he got the implication, but he didn't say anything. "He said he had a buyer who had purchased everything he had, which was why he couldn't sell any of it to Sam. What if that lot included letter openers? That would have made it easy enough for him to replace."

"I suppose there's only one way to find out," Richard said, sounding just a tad bit disgruntled about it. "We'll have to ask Gary directly."

"This could be the solution you're looking for. Perhaps then I could finally get my invitation to dinner?"

He smiled at that, but there was something inscrutable in his eyes.

"Once again, good detective work, Penelope."

"Thank you, Richard," she said, feeling pleased.

CHAPTER TWENTY-SIX

The next morning, Detective and Penelope darkened the front doors of the Grand Opal Hotel with their presence yet again. Much to Wendell Dickens' dismay.

"Detective Prescott," he said in a terse tone as he rushed over to them. He cast a hard gaze upon Penelope. "Miss Banks. I thought it was made clear to you that you were no longer—"

"We're here to speak to Gary Garret, *officially*," Detective Prescott said in a harsh tone, cutting him off. "Is he still employed?"

They had tried Gary at his apartment to find that he wasn't home. The hotel had seemed like the obvious next stop.

"He is," Wendell said, looking put out by that fact. "We've had a recent onslaught of staff quitting for some reason, so we had no choice but to keep him on."

Penelope held back a smile, glad that Rosie had spread the word about the financial troubles.

Wendell sniffed and straightened up. "I will escort you down to the *staff* area. You can interview him *there*."

Rather than wait for the staff elevator, which they all knew would take a while, he led them to the stairwell.

"One question, while I have you," Detective Prescott asked. "The letter openers. Would Mr. Combs have had access to them prior to his stay here? Perhaps when he was consulting? Maybe one was gifted to him?"

Wendell frowned. "I don't see how. His services were limited to the larger details of the look and feel of the hotel, and helping coordinate our connections with Japan." Pen and Detective Prescott eyed each other at that statement. "The rooms weren't even supplied until just prior to the first suite guests arriving. As far as gifting one, he most certainly was not. Such a paltry gift would have been an insult."

"One more question. Who was in charge of shipments from Japan?"

"I was," Wendell said proudly.

Penelope and Detective Prescott cast another look at each other. If he had anything to do with this test shipment, he was either incredibly stupid to admit such a thing...or he had no idea he was being used by someone else.

"Just you? Who decided on which shipping company to use? Where to source products? Things like that? Was Mr. Combs involved to that degree?"

"Well, er, Miss Walton left it up to me to delegate. While I certainly had the final say, I did get input from him, yes."

This time when Penelope met the detective's eyes she could see the same satisfaction she felt running through her. They really were close to solving this case.

MURDER IN THE GARDENS

In the basement staff area, they found Gary chatting with a bellhop in uniform.

"Mr. Garret," Wendell said in a curt voice. "These two would like a word."

Gary stared at them, understandably wary at Detective Prescott's presence.

"Thank you, Mr. Dickens," Detective Prescott said in a dismissive tone.

Wendell tightened his mouth with displeasure, glared at Gary for bringing this bit of unpleasantness to the hotel, then promptly left. The bellhop also wisely departed, quickly leaving the area so they had privacy.

"Don't worry," Pen assured Gary. "We're just here to ask you for information about someone else."

"Anything I can do to help."

"That lot of surplus you got your hands on during the construction of this hotel," Pen began. That did nothing to settle Gary, who shot a look of alarm toward Detective Prescott. She gave Detective Prescott a pointed look. "Don't worry about him. He fully plans on ignoring that tiny bit of malfeasance."

"What did you want to know?" Gary asked, definitely still on guard.

"Who was it that bought the lot?"

"Hubert Combs," he shot Penelope a guilty look. "I didn't say anything before out of professional courtesy to him. I try to be discreet in my dealings. Does it have something to do with the case? If I'd known, I would have said something."

"Never mind that," Detective Prescott interjected in a terse voice, drawing his attention back.

"He's still up in the Oriental Suite if that helps?"

"He's still here?" Pen said in surprise.

247

"I'm sure of it."

"And this lot, did it include the letter openers?"

"It did."

"Do you remember how many there were in the lot exactly?"

"Ten of them. I remember because they came bundled in packs of ten. I only swiped one pack. I figured that would be something they'd miss, so I didn't take any more than that."

Pen shot Detective Prescott a satisfied smile. He gave her a conceding smile in return, then turned to Gary again.

"Did he mention why he wanted to buy the whole lot of everything you had?"

Gary shrugged. "Just said he didn't want anyone else getting their hands on it."

"Nothing more than that?"

"I wasn't asking too many questions considering how much he paid me," Gary said with a guilty smile.

"Right," Detective Prescott said, mulling that information over. Pen studied him to see if there was anything else he needed from Gary. Finally, he exhaled. "I suppose that's all, Mr. Garret. Thank you for your help."

The two of them left, heading back to the stairs.

"That's odd isn't it?" Pen said. "Why would Hubert be interested in keeping anyone else from getting supplies from this hotel?"

"We're about to find out." Detective Prescott led Pen back to the front desk instead, again to Wendell's dismay.

"What is it now?" He asked testily, his professionalism exhausted.

"Mr. Hubert Combs, he is still a guest, correct?"

"He is," Wendell said, thoroughly unhappy at what this was obviously leading to.

"We will need to talk to him," Detective Prescott said with an insistent smile.

Wendell closed his eyes at this bane on his day. "Very well, I'll escort you myself."

"We can find the way. The Oriental Suite, no?"

Wendell frowned but gave him a curt nod. "Can I at least ask for your discretion should...any unpleasantness ensue?"

"I'll do my best."

Detective Prescott and Pen went to the elevators, exchanging grins. Once inside, she turned to him.

"I'm surprised you're including me in this part."

"You have a certain value as it turns out. The making of a good investigator. You might notice things I don't."

Pen smiled, feeling pleased.

"I suggest we start by questioning why he bought the entire lot. Don't mention the letter openers. Let's see what his excuse is."

Penelope nodded. He was more of an expert than she, so she didn't argue.

When they arrived on the sixteenth floor, they stepped off and knocked on the door to the Oriental Suite.

Just as last time, Hubert opened the door only a crack. He studied them through narrowed eyes. "Back again? How is it I can help you this time?"

"I had a few more questions regarding the investigation." Before Hubert could simply close the door on them, he added. "We have a suspect we're looking at and we need you to clarify a few things for us, if you don't mind."

Technically the truth.

Penelope could see the instant curiosity in his eyes. Detective Prescott had planted the seed in his head that he might inadvertently learn more about how the case was proceeding. It was smart, and it made her admire him all the more.

"Very well," Hubert said, opening the door for them. He was once again dressed in his robe and he led them to the couch. "What is it you would like to know?"

"I understand you were an advisor during the construction of this hotel?"

"I was," Hubert said cautiously.

"Did you notice anything suspicious during that time? Or anything unusual with anyone? Say, Wendell Dickens or Gary Garrett, or anyone else, perhaps even Genevieve Walton or Jiro Ishida?"

Hubert visibly relaxed, realizing this was simply a fishing expedition. "There's always something odd or unusual going on in an endeavor of this size. Nothing gets done in this city without a few palms getting greased, if you know what I mean."

Detective Prescott breathed out a humorless laugh. "Unfortunately, I do. Speaking of which, why is it you bought the lot of surplus materials Gary Garret had pilfered?"

Hubert blinked in surprise. It took a moment for him to recover, his eyes finally narrowing with amused resentment.

"I suppose at this point, there's no harm in revealing my plans."

Both Penelope and Detective Prescott sat up straighter.

"I plan on purchasing this hotel. For much less than it's worth, of course. I saw the folly in how Genevieve was spending money so recklessly, and I wasn't the only one."

"Takashi Ando?" Penelope asked.

"My, my, you two have been busy."

"So you have a connection with Mr. Ando?" Detective Prescott confirmed.

"Anyone doing business with Japan does."

"That's why you secretly bought all the surplus materials from Mr. Garret," Pen said. "You didn't want any competition getting their hands on what would soon be yours."

He studied her with a narrow-eyed gaze. "Correct."

Beside her, Detective Prescott leaned in, and she knew he was about to go in for the kill. "And that included exactly ten letter openers with the hotel logo."

Hubert Combs paused, taken by surprise. "I don't recall exactly what was included."

"That's irrelevant. We know from the source that exactly ten were included in the lot that you purchased. We will be getting a warrant to search every property that you own in search of that lot. I suspect it's someplace close though, close enough for you to quickly rush out and get a replacement for your hotel suite, being that you used yours to kill Mandy Clarkson. In fact, I think maybe you brought it ahead of time, knowing you would use yours to kill her. That's premeditation, Mr. Combs."

"You have no proof of that!" he exclaimed.

He was panicked and agitated, which was a sure sign that they had homed in on his guilt.

"Is it because she discovered your little plan for shipping opium? We already know that the azalea tree was simply a test run for future shipments. You and Bentley Green coordinated this together, didn't you? And with these hotels he's helping build around the country, each with their own Japanese garden, that gives you every opportunity to ship even more without looking suspicious."

Now Hubert was even whiter.

"How did you—?" He stopped himself before he gave too much away. Once again he recovered. "I think it's time for you to leave."

Detective Prescott stayed seated, giving Hubert a hard look. "Mr. Combs, right now *everything* is tied to you: Mandy's murder, the plan to ship opium, your shady ties to Japan, which I'm sure the federal government will take an active interest in. As far as I'm concerned, Jiro Ishida's death is also on your hands."

"*Jiro?* I didn't kill him!"

"You had every reason to," Penelope pressed. "Takashi Ando's interest in Jiro was having a connection to America, someone who understood Japanese culture but was also a citizen. With him out of the way, you fit that bill even better."

"Exactly! Jiro was no competition for me. He wasn't even willing to participate, but I was! Furthermore, as a white man, I didn't face the same prejudices and obstacles he would have. I had no reason to kill him."

"Face it, Mr. Combs, it wouldn't take much for a jury to decide that you would kill, not just one, but two people involved in this to protect your secret; that's an instant death penalty verdict. However, we can make the case that perhaps Jiro's death was an accident, that's simple manslaughter. You might be out in fifteen years. But when you combine it with Mandy's death that's a coordinated plan. No one would believe you just happened to kill two people by accident."

"No! I see what you're doing. You have no proof I killed Jiro because I didn't do it! As for Mandy...again, it's all circumstantial."

"If you tell us who your accomplice was you might be able to cut a deal with the prosecutor. Murder is a serious crime. Manslaughter, less so. But I do know he would happily give you immunity if you were to help curb an illegal opium smuggling conspiracy. They take that business very seriously."

"If you're looking for a culprit there, Bentley Green is the most obvious one," he spat with a harsh laugh. "In fact, I'll bet he was the one who killed Jiro—and Mandy for that matter," he added less convincingly.

"Do you have any proof of that?" Detective Prescott asked.

"It's well known that he has a taste for that stuff," Hubert spat. "Mandy was the one to go to *his* suite that night, not even realizing what she had—or rather didn't have. She probably stayed long after he plied her with who knows what, like he does all his little tarts."

Penelope felt her heart quicken. She wondered if Detective Prescott had heard the same thing that she had. He was good at his job, so she was sure of it. Hubert Combs had just foisted himself on his own petard.

"How do you know she went to his suite?" Detective Prescott said, easily luring Hubert further into his own trap, or at least into giving them more information about who was involved.

Hubert looked caught off guard.

"I...I heard her." Something seemed to occur to him and he gave them a piercing look. "In fact, *Bentley* was the only one she had any association with. I never so much as talked to the little trollop. *He's* the one you want. He has all the connections here in New York when it comes to opium. *He* was the one who had plans to build future hotels around the country, each with a Japanese garden, as you said. Which would have included bonsai trees, in case you needed someone to spell everything out for you."

253

"You make a good case," Detective Prescott said. "But I need more than just your say so."

Penelope smiled to herself. She knew exactly what Detective Prescott was doing. They had Hubert for Mandy's murder based on the letter openers—combined with the fact that he knew the azalea tree didn't actually have opium at its base. But, they needed a coconspirator for Jiro's death. And Hubert was the most likely to give them a suspect.

"Oh for heaven's sakes, detective! Just how incompetent are you? Everyone knows that Bentley is involved with opium."

"How did *you* know that? My understanding is, it was a fairly close kept secret."

"The way anyone knows these things. It's gossip! Even the staff here knew, they know everything. I learned early on in life that their ears pick up every little tidbit, all while their betters are inclined to treat them as nothing more than docile little pets."

"You're still not giving me anything that could possibly hold up in court, Mr. Combs."

Hubert held firm for a moment, then seemed to sag. "Fine, I couldn't have killed Jiro because I was with someone at the time. Are you happy?"

Penelope blinked in surprise. "With whom?"

Hubert sniffed and sat up straighter. "One of the bellboys here and I share certain...interests."

Ah," Penelope said with understanding. "As in the kind of interests that don't involve the fairer sex?"

Hubert went a shade whiter and swallowed hard. "I didn't want to involve him but it seems it's necessary at this point. Stanley is his name. I hope that you will be *discreet* when questioning him?"

Penelope and Detective Prescott glanced at each other. There was an unspoken bit of communication between them. They both turned back to Hubert.

"We can certainly keep this discreet, despite the laws against certain things like that. But we need to know about your involvement in this opium business."

"It was all Bentley's idea," he said in a despondent tone. "As I said, *he* has the connection here in New York, and with this contract for all these hotels, it would have been too easy to import from Asia. That's where he needed me. All I did was get him in touch with Mr. Ando," He insisted, then frowned. "Then this *Mandy* comes along to throw a monkey wrench into the entire works. Bentley thought he could appease her with dresses and promises of a better life. I knew better. The lower classes are like rats. They've learned to survive through devious means, nibbling their way into things, never fully satisfied. Much like with vermin, *I* knew she had to be dealt with."

Now, Pen didn't feel bad at all about the bit of blackmail they were using against him. Hubert was just as much a horrid snob as she'd first assumed at the party.

"At least Jiro had a certain degree of civility. Being Japanese, that's understandable. His death truly is a loss. One which I had no hand in. All the same, I couldn't very well have you all looking too closely into the circumstances surrounding his murder."

"So you're the one who had the case hushed up," Detective Prescott confirmed.

Hubert nodded then looked off to the side thoughtfully. "It's not illegal, you know—opium, that is. Doctors prescribe it every day, or at least a variant of it. And more than a few of our city's wealthier patriarchs have padded their fortunes by dealing in it. Those names you see on various buildings and funding one charitable cause or another? Their hands are no less dirty than mine. It does work wonders when it comes to pain. That's how Bentley got addicted in the first place. A simple tumble down the stairs and a resulting bad knee."

Detective Prescott cleared his throat to get Hubert's attention. "Mr. Combs, I'm afraid I'm going to have to place you under arrest for the murder of Mandy Clarkson."

Hubert gave him a soft smile and nodded. "I suppose it was only a matter of time before the facade was exposed. I'm surprised it took you so long to find her body."

"The staff elevator is notoriously slow," Pen muttered, almost to herself. She was lost in thought. Something about what Hubert said nagged at her:

I suppose it was only a matter of time before the facade was exposed.

"Zounds!" She finally exclaimed. That had both men turning to her with questioning looks.

She stared back at them feeling her heart race. "I think I know who was with Mandy when Jiro was murdered."

CHAPTER TWENTY-SEVEN

"Time," Penelope said as she rode the elevator down with Detective Prescott and Hubert Combs. He had used the phone in the Oriental Suite to call the police to come and take Hubert away once they were in the lobby. He had also graciously allowed Hubert to change into something more appropriate than the robe he had on.

"Time?" The detective repeated.

"Yes. It didn't add up. And when Hubert here mentioned a facade it all fell into place."

"Care to tell me what?"

"Not quite yet. Once the police come and take Mr. Combs away, I need to have another chat with someone in this hotel."

To his credit, Detective Prescott simply nodded and accepted that Penelope knew what she was talking about.

Once in the lobby, it didn't take long for the police to arrive. Wendell Dickens scowled at them while they waited, but he knew better than to intervene. Now that it seemed they had a suspect, he knew the case, and thus his headache, would soon be over.

Little did he know...

Once Hubert was in handcuffs and taken away, Detective Prescott turned to Pen with an expectant look.

"Follow me," she said, heading back into the hotel...

...past the front desk...

...past the main elevators...

...past the staff elevator...

...and to the stairs.

Instead of going up, they went down.

Pen led him through the staff area and straight to where they had left Gary earlier.

"Miss Banks," he said, with a half-cocked smile. "Back again?"

He must have seen the way she stared at him because his smile faded. "What is it?"

"I know it was you with Mandy that night. You were with her on the roof when she killed Jiro."

"What?" he said with a nervous laugh. "No, I went up after the fact, Jiro was already dead when I got there."

"You did go back, but it was to find your missing button...after you had helped her drown Jiro."

His jaw hardened. "That's not true."

"It is," she said, feeling her resentment set in. She hated that she had believed in his innocence. "You told me you went straight to the roof after Mandy interrupted the card game."

He didn't answer at first. "I may have not gone up immediately."

"Then where were you? Did anyone see you?"

He didn't respond, but she could see the anger and panic brewing in his gaze.

"You went up with Mandy after she discovered there might be opium hidden at the base of the azalea tree, no?

MURDER IN THE GARDENS

She knew you had connections and would probably know who could help her sell it. In fact, you were the one to tell Bobby Paxton that Bentley Green could help him get a hold of some opium, weren't you?"

He remained silent. By now, she knew she wasn't getting a response from him, so she continued.

"But Jiro Ishida made an unexpected appearance. I'm sure it was an accident, but either you or Mandy panicked. He somehow hit his head, but he was only dazed at that point. But he'd discovered what you were up to. You certainly couldn't leave a witness, especially when it came to something like opium. You had to get rid of him. Still, you at least tried to make it look like an accident."

Something occurred to Pen and she felt her heart sink even more.

"In fact, I think the drowning was all you. Rosie ran into Mandy getting cleaning supplies to clean the trail of blood. When she related the story back to me she said nothing about her being wet at the time, which is something that she definitely would have mentioned. You were the only one who was wet, dripping water and dirt down the stairwell as you took the tree down to the Bridal Suite while Mandy cleaned up."

Gary just sat back in his chair, studying her, expressionless.

"When Mandy was finished, her uniform was probably covered in blood and dirt. Something that definitely would have been remarked on. So she changed into Rosie's uniform, knowing she had gone home already.

"At some point, you noticed the missing button from your shirt. It made sense that it had probably come off during the struggle to drown Jiro, so you quickly rushed back up to look for it, knowing it would tie you to the crime."

A humorless smile came to her lips. "You were probably quite surprised to find him no longer in the pond, weren't you? Despite telling me you had pulled him out, supposedly to see if you could rescue him."

Next to her, Detective Prescott exhaled in astonishment.

Pen turned to him with a dry smile. "When Betty had mentioned Jiro's eyes staring back at her, like me you probably assumed she had meant she'd seen them in her head. But Betty had in fact managed to pull Jiro out of the pond. His lifeless eyes really were literally staring at her when the elevator doors closed on her."

"So there was no reason for Mr. Garret to be so wet." He turned to Gary. "Since you weren't really rescuing Mr. Ishida, you were searching in the water for your button."

Gary's face gave away nothing, and Pen shook her head. "You really are quite the formidable poker player, Gary. Such a waste. Rosie was right, you really could give Valentino a run for his money. That act in the lobby? I actually believed it."

Penelope couldn't bear to look at Gary, even to finish spelling out the crime. Richard, next to her seemed to sense it so he continued in her stead.

"I'm guessing when Mr. Dickens arrived on the roof after Mrs. Paxton called him, you had to think quickly. You were wet and you knew a button of yours was missing. So you pretended that you had been trying to rescue him."

They both waited, but Gary said nothing.

"It is your right to remain silent. But you are still under arrest for murder, Gary Garret. I wouldn't expect anyone to make a phone call this time around to get you out of jail. I suspect the person who intervened last time will be too busy saving his own neck."

Detective Prescott met Penelope's eyes as he forced Gary to his feet.

"Good detective work...Penelope."

All she could manage was the barest hint of a smile. This hadn't been a happy ending.

EPILOGUE

"They've set a trial date for Bentley Green," Jane announced.

Penelope was in the office with her associate, the two of them partaking in their usual morning routine of reading the morning paper. Penelope had been paying particularly close attention to the national and world news. This case had taught her the importance of being well-versed in both.

"Good, it's about time that entire nasty business was put to rest. I'm sure the prosecutor is thrilled to have such a high-profile case, all while stamping out a part of the opium trade."

Hubert Combs had pleaded guilty to a lesser charge of the manslaughter of Mandy Clarkson rather than face court under a murder charge. He had officially confessed that he had killed Mandy not only for discovering his opium conspiracy with Bentley but also out of anger at suspecting she had killed Jiro Ishida, whom he admired. He'd put her in the staff elevator merely out of convenience, not realizing how irregularly they were used. He had also agreed to testify against Bentley Green for his part in the opium conspiracy.

Gary Garret was taking his chances with a trial. Unfortunately for him, there was already a stream of witnesses to attest to the timeline of events and what had happened, including Betty Paxton and Penelope Banks. He had even lost whatever charm he had in Rosie's eyes, who would also be a witness against him. Murder had a tainting effect on one's attraction.

Jiro Ishida was becoming quite popular after his death. Visits to his final work of art atop the Grand Opal Hotel now had waiting lists. Not that it helped the bottom line of the hotel any. Penelope had learned from her father—who she was slowly warming to more and more—that the Sinclairs were in the works to purchase it from Genevieve. The name would of course change, but hopefully, they'd maintain the eastern charm it held.

With help from Betty Paxton, Penelope had gotten in touch with Jiro Ishida's family and offered to pay whatever amount they needed to escape Japan. Obviously, America had lost any appeal for them, not that it was an option considering the new immigration laws. Instead, they'd decided on Brazil, where quite a few Japanese ex-pats had made a new home.

As for the Paxtons, it seemed Robert Lee had played his last professional game the week of Jiro's and Mandy's murders. Despite performing abysmally and not winning the tournament, Bobby had been in surprisingly good spirits after the game. Penelope could only surmise just how much he had bet against himself. It must have been quite the sum.

"I'll only be happy when all is said and done and everyone is finally reaping what they sowed," Pen said with a sigh.

MURDER IN THE GARDENS

Jane gave her a sympathetic look. "Are you still upset over it, Miss Banks?"

"Not at all," she scoffed. "Oh, alright, perhaps a bit resentful. It seems I have a weakness for attractive, charming men. One would have thought I'd learned my lesson with Clifford."

Perhaps Richard was right about waiting to ask her to dinner. Whatever these mysterious "affairs" he had to get in order were, she preferred that they didn't create problems after she'd already fallen for him—at least more than she already had.

"At least you finally got a new maid out of it, no?" Jane said, trying to cheer her up. "Your cousin must be happy about that."

Penelope laughed. "Rosie's already got a job working for The Plaza, apparently she missed having other maids to work alongside."

"I can understand that. I certainly enjoy working with you."

"I agree, it is nice having someone to work alongside," Penelope said with an appreciative smile. "In fact, let's put all this investigative business on hold for today. Spring is still lingering in the air, and I say we enjoy it."

"What do you mean?"

"I mean, let's get out of the office," Pen said, tossing her own paper on her desk. "I'm taking you on a trip to the Botanical Gardens. I can show you some of Jiro Ishida's other work. I'd rather honor his memory that way. Let's turn this case into a happy ending after all."

Jane gave her a smile of approval. "I think Mr. Ishida would appreciate that, Miss Banks."

CONTINUE ON FOR YOUR FREE BOOK!

AUTHOR'S NOTE

The main branch of the Brooklyn Public Library has a small section of non-circulating books dedicated to New York History. Obviously, this is a favorite haunt of mine. One book in particular includes little asides in the margins of the book, usually quotes or facts from the time period covered. The following passage was taken from a quote by F. Scott Fitzgerald:

From the confusion of the year 1920, I remember riding on top of a taxi-cab along deserted Fifth Avenue on a hot Sunday night, and a luncheon in the cool Japanese gardens at the Ritz...

Not to dismiss Fitzgerald and his fascinating, whimsical remembrances, but the part that really caught my eye was the bit about the Ritz Carlton. Obviously, I had to know more (yes, I did wonder at "riding on top of a taxi-cab," but I may save that banana oil for another book).

As it turns out, the Ritz wasn't the only game in town to sport a Japanese garden. The Astor Hotel, which no longer exists, also opened one in 1923 (according to a New York Times article published March 4 of that year) to some

AUTHOR'S NOTE

fanfare. In fact, it was that hotel that inspired this book. It was designed by Takeo Shiota, who also designed the Japanese garden in the Brooklyn Botanical Gardens (pardon my artistic license in name change there).

Two hotels were enough for yours truly to consider it "all the rage," at least in Penelope Banks' version of the 1920s. It was good fun teaching myself about Japanese tea gardens and applying the information here.

With the victim being of Japanese heritage, I thought it only fair to accurately incorporate the ethos of the day. The Immigration Act of 1924 was rightfully labeled the Asian Exclusion Act because it did just that.

Prior to this act, the Japanese had a Gentleman's Agreement with the United States to limit immigration, while not expressly barring the Japanese from becoming citizens. The 1924 Act effectively terminated this agreement, and some cite it as one of the initial sparks that eventually led to Japan's involvement in WWII. I leave that to the geo-political historians to pontificate. For yours truly, it was a fascinating history assignment.

As for the opium trade, in my research I did learn that at least one famously wealthy turn of the century baron—yes, whose name you may find on a few buildings and attached to various charitable causes—had made part of his fortune dealing opium in China of all places. To protect the guilty, I shall not name names.

CONTINUE ON FOR YOUR FREE BOOK!

GET YOUR FREE BOOK!

Mischief at The Peacock Club

A bold theft at the infamous Peacock Club. Can Penelope solve it to save her own neck?

1924 New York
Penelope "Pen" Banks has spent the past two years making ends meet by playing cards. It's another Saturday night at The Peacock Club, one of her favorite haunts, and she has

GET YOUR FREE BOOK!

her sites set on a big fish, who just happens to be the special guest of the infamous Jack Sweeney.

After inducing Rupert Cartland, into a game of cards, Pen thinks it just might be her lucky night. Unfortunately, before the night ends, Rupert has been robbed—his diamond cuff links, ruby pinky ring, gold watch, and wallet...all gone!

With The Peacock Club's reputation on the line, Mr. Sweeney, aided by the heavy hand of his chief underling Tommy Callahan, is holding everyone captive until the culprit is found.

For the promise of a nice payoff, not to mention escaping the club in one piece, Penelope Banks is willing to put her unique mind to work to find out just who stole the goods.

This is a prequel novella to the *Penelope Banks Murder Mysteries* series, taking place at The Peacock Club before Penelope Banks became a private investigator.

Access your book at the link below:
https://dl.bookfunnel.com/4sv9fir4h3

ALSO BY COLETTE CLARK

PENELOPE BANKS MURDER MYSTERIES

A Murder in Long Island

The Missing White Lady

Pearls, Poison & Park Avenue

Murder in the Gardens

A Murder in Washington Square

The Great Gaston Murder

A Murder After Death

A Murder on 34th Street

LISETTE DARLING GOLDEN AGE MYSTERIES

A Sparkling Case of Murder

ABOUT THE AUTHOR

Colette Clark lives in New York and has always enjoyed learning more about the history of her amazing city. She decided to combine that curiosity and love of learning with her addiction to reading and watching mysteries. Her first series, **Penelope Banks Murder Mysteries** is the result of those passions. When she's not writing she can be found doing Sudoku puzzles, drawing, eating tacos, visiting museums dedicated to unusual/weird/wacky things, and, of course, reading mysteries by other great authors.

Join my Newsletter to receive news about New Releases and Sales!
https://dashboard.mailerlite.com/forms/148684/726783564877767318/share

Printed in Great Britain
by Amazon